“What would you do if you were mine?”

The question caught her off guard while her brain zipped off on a disorienting, romantic tangent. To be Tuck’s. In his arms. In his life. In his bed.

“Sorry?” She scrambled to bring her thoughts back to the real world.

“If you were my confidential assistant, what would you do?”

“I’m not.” She wasn’t his anything, and she had to remember that.

“But if you were?”

If she were Tuck’s assistant, she’d be in the middle of making one colossal mistake. Eventually, she would kiss her boss. She was thinking about it right now. And if the dusky smoke in his eyes was anything to go by, he was thinking about it, too.

* * *

A Bargain with the Boss is part of the Chicago Sons series—Men who work hard, love harder and live with their fathers’ legacies...

Dear Reader,

Welcome to book three of the Chicago Sons series! I've worked in a lot of offices over the years and observed a lot of office romances. It's a great place to meet people, and an even better place to get to know their inner character—such as a love of animals, a flair for gourmet cooking, or a passion for shoes.

Tuck Tucker appeared in the first two Chicago Sons stories and quickly became one of my favorites for a future hero. He's been a public face for Tucker Transportation for many years, with his brother running the company. He's inept and intimidated by the day-to-day business. So, who better to throw in his path than Amber Bowen, office manager extraordinaire? She's smart, hardworking and buttoned-down—with the sexiest shoe collection in greater Chicago. She'll keep Tuck on the straight and narrow, or he'll pull her off.

Happy reading. I hope you enjoy *A Bargain with the Boss*!

Barbara

A BARGAIN WITH THE BOSS

BARBARA DUNLOP

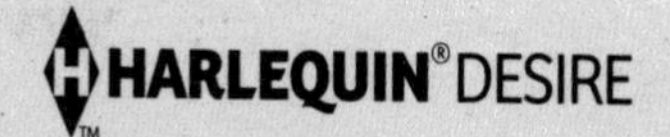

ISBN-13: 978-0-373-73453-5

A Bargain with the Boss

This edition published by arrangement with Harlequin Books S.A.

For questions and comments about the quality of this book, please contact us at CustomerService@Harlequin.com.

Printed in U.S.A.

Barbara Dunlop writes romantic stories while curled up in a log cabin in Canada's far north, where bears outnumber people and it snows six months of the year. Fortunately she has a brawny husband and two teenage children to haul firewood and clear the driveway while she sips cocoa and muses about her upcoming chapters. Barbara loves to hear from readers. You can contact her through her website, barbaradunlop.com.

Books by Barbara Dunlop

HARLEQUIN DESIRE

An After-Hours Affair
A Golden Betrayal
A Conflict of Interest
The Missing Heir
The Baby Contract

Colorado Cattle Barons

A Cowboy Comes Home
A Cowboy in Manhattan
An Intimate Bargain
Millionaire in a Stetson
A Cowboy's Temptation
The Last Cowboy Standing

Chicago Sons

Sex, Lies and the CEO
Seduced by the CEO
A Bargain with the Boss

Visit her Author Profile page at Harlequin.com, or barbaradunlop.com, for more titles!

Thanks to Kieran Slobodin for the title.

And thanks to Shona Mostyn and
Brittany Pearson for the shoes!

One

Saturday night ended early for Lawrence "Tuck" Tucker. His date had not gone well.

Her name was Felicity. She had a bright smile, sunshine-blond hair, a body that could stop traffic and the IQ of a basset hound. But she also had a shrill, long-winded conversational style, and she was stridently against subsidized day care and team sports for children. Plus, she hated the Bulls. What self-respecting Chicagoan hated the Bulls? That was just disloyal.

By the time they'd finished dessert, Tuck was tired of being lectured in high C. He decided life was too short, so he'd dropped her off at her apartment with a fleeting good-night kiss.

Now he let himself into the expansive foyer of the Tucker family mansion, shifting his thoughts ahead to Sunday morning. He was meeting his friend Shane Colborn for, somewhat ironically, a pickup basketball game.

"That's just *reckless*." The angry voice of his father, Jamison Tucker, rang clearly from the library.

"I'm not saying it'll be easy," said Tuck's older brother, Dixon, his own voice tight with frustration.

Together the two men ran the family's multinational conglomerate, Tucker Transportation, and it was highly unusual for them to argue.

"Now, *that's* an understatement," said Jamison. "Who could possibly step in? I'm tied up. And we're not sending some junior executive to Antwerp."

"The operations director is not a junior executive."

"We need a vice president to represent the company. We need you."

"Then, send Tuck."

"Tuck?" Jamison scoffed.

The derision in his father's voice shouldn't have bothered Tuck. But it did. Even after all these years, he still felt the sting in his father's lack of faith and respect.

"He's a vice president," said Dixon.

"In name only. And barely that."

"Dad—"

"Don't you *Dad* me. You know your brother's shortcomings as well as I do. You want to take an extended vacation? *Now?*"

"I didn't choose the timing."

Jamison's voice moderated. "She did you wrong, son. Everybody knows that."

"My wife of ten years betrayed every promise we ever made to each other. Do you have any idea how that feels?"

Tuck's sympathies went out to Dixon. It had been a terrible few months since Dixon had caught Kassandra in bed with another man. The final divorce papers had arrived earlier this week. Dixon hadn't said much about them. In fact, he'd been unusually tight-lipped.

"And you're angry. And that's fine. But you bested her in the divorce. We held up the prenup and she's walking away with next to nothing."

All emotion left Dixon's voice. "It's all about the money to you, isn't it?"

"It was to her," said Jamison.

There was a break in the conversation, and Tuck realized they could easily emerge from the library and catch him eavesdropping. He took a silent step back toward the front door.

"Tuck deserves a chance," said Dixon.

Tuck froze again to listen.

"Tuck had a chance," said Jamison, his words stinging once again.

When? Tuck wanted to shout. When had he had a chance to do anything but sit in his executive floor office and feel like an unwanted guest?

But as quickly as the emotion formed, he reminded himself that he didn't care. His only defense against his father was not to care about respect or recognition or making any meaningful contribution to the family business. Most people would kill for Tuck's lifestyle. He needed to shut up and enjoy it.

"I knew this was a bad idea," said Dixon.

"It was a terrible idea," said Jamison.

Tuck reached behind himself and opened the front door. Then he shut it hard, making a show of tromping his feet over the hardwood floor.

"Hello?" he called out as he walked toward the library, giving them ample time to pretend they'd been talking about something else.

"Hi, Tuck." His brother greeted him as he entered the dark-hued, masculine room.

"I didn't see your car out front," Tuck told him.

"I parked it in the garage."

"So you're staying over?"

Dixon had a penthouse downtown, where he'd lived with Kassandra, but he occasionally spent a day or two at the family home.

"I'm staying over," said Dixon. "I sold the penthouse today."

From the expression on his father's face, Tuck could tell this was news to him, as well.

"So you'll be here for a while?" Tuck asked easily. He loosened his tie and pulled it off. "What are you drinking?"

"Glen Garron," Jamison answered.

"Sounds good." Tuck shrugged out of his jacket and tossed it onto one of the deep red leather wingback chairs.

With a perimeter of ceiling-high shelves, a stone fireplace, oversize leather chairs and ornately carved walnut tables, the library hadn't changed in seventy years. It had been built by Tuck's grandfather, Randal, as a gentleman's retreat, back in the days when gentlemen thought they had something to retreat from.

Tuck didn't fill the silence, but instead waited to see where his father and brother would take the conversation.

"How was your date?" his father asked.

"It was fine."

Jamison looked pointedly at his heavy platinum watch.

"She wasn't exactly a rocket scientist," Tuck said, answering the unspoken question.

"You've dated a rocket scientist?" asked Jamison.

Tuck frowned at his father's mocking tone.

The two men locked gazes for a moment before Jamison spoke. "I merely wondered how you had a basis for comparison."

"First date?" Dixon queried, his tone much less judgmental.

Tuck crossed to the wet bar and flipped up a cut crystal glass. "Last date."

Dixon gave a chopped laugh.

Tuck poured a measure of scotch. "Interested in the game with Shane tomorrow?" he asked his brother.

"Can't," said Dixon.

"Work?" asked Tuck.

"Tying up loose ends."

Tuck turned to face the other men. "With the penthouse?"

Dixon's expression was inscrutable. "And a few other things."

Tuck got the distinct feeling Dixon was holding something back. But then the two brothers rarely spoke frankly in front of their father. Tuck would catch up with Dixon at some point tomorrow and ask him what was going on. Was he really looking at taking a lengthy vacation? Tuck would be impressed if he was.

Then again, their father was right. Tucker Transportation needed Dixon to keep the corporation running at full speed. And Tuck wasn't any kind of a substitute on that front.

Amber Bowen looked straight into the eyes of the president of Tucker Transportation and lied.

"No," she said to Jamison Tucker. "Dixon didn't mention anything to me."

Her loyalty was to her boss, Dixon Tucker. Five years ago, he'd given her a chance when nobody else would. She'd been straight out of high school, with no college education and no office experience. He'd put his faith in her then, and she wasn't going to let him down now.

"When was the last time you spoke to him?"

Jamison Tucker was an imposing figure behind his big desk in the corner office on the thirty-second floor of the Tucker Transportation building. His gray hair was neat, freshly cut every three weeks. His suit was custom-made to cover his barrel chest. He wasn't as tall as his two sons, but he more than made up for it in sturdiness. He was thick necked, like a bulldog. His brow was heavy and his face was square.

"Yesterday morning," said Amber. This time she was telling the truth.

His eyes narrowed with what looked like suspicion. "You didn't see him last night, sometime after the office closed?"

The question took her aback. "I… Why?"

"It's a yes-or-no answer, Amber."

"No."

Why would Jamison ask that question, and why in such a suspicious tone?

"Are you sure?" Jamison asked her, skepticism in his pale blue eyes.

She hesitated before answering. "Do you have some reason to believe I saw him last night?"

"*Did* you see him last night?" There was a note of triumph in his voice.

She hadn't. But she did know where Dixon had been last night. He was at the airport, boarding a private jet for Arizona. She knew he'd left Chicago, and she knew he wouldn't be back for a very long time.

He'd told her he'd left a note for his family so they wouldn't worry. And he'd made her promise not to give anyone more information. And she was keeping that promise.

Dixon's family took shameless advantage of his good nature

and his strong work ethic. The result was that he was overworked and exhausted. He'd been doing an increasing share of the senior management duties at Tucker Transportation over the past couple of years. And now his divorce had taken a huge toll on his mental and emotional state. If he didn't get some help soon, he was headed for a breakdown.

She knew he'd tried to explain it to his family. She also knew they refused to listen. He'd had no choice but to simply disappear. His father and his lazy, good-for-nothing younger brother, Tuck, were simply going to have to step up.

She squared her shoulders. "Are you implying that I have a personal relationship with Dixon?"

Jamison leaned slightly forward. "I don't imply."

"Yes, you do. You did." She knew she was skating on thin ice, but she was angry on her behalf and Dixon's. It was Dixon's wife who had cheated, not Dixon.

Jamison's tone went lower. "How dare you?"

"How dare you, sir. Have some faith in your own son."

Then Jamison's eyes seemed to bulge. His complexion turned ruddy. "Why, you—"

Amber braced herself, gripping the arm of the chair, afraid she would be fired on the spot. She could only hope Dixon would hire her back when he returned.

But Jamison gasped instead and his hand went to his chest. His body stiffened in the big chair and he sucked in three short breaths.

Amber shot to her feet. "Mr. Tucker?"

There was genuine terror in his expression.

She grabbed the desk phone, calling out to his assistant as she dialed 911.

Jamison's assistant, Margaret Smithers, was through the door in a flash.

While Amber gave instructions to the emergency operator, Margaret called the company nurse.

Within minutes, the nurse had Jamison on his back on the floor of his office and was administering CPR.

Amber watched the scene in horror. Had his heart truly stopped? Was he going to die right here in the office?

She knew she should get word to his family. His wife needed to know what had happened. Then again, Mrs. Tucker probably shouldn't be alone when she heard. She probably shouldn't hear news like this from a company secretary.

"I need to call Tuck," Amber said to Margaret.

All the blood had drained from Margaret's face. She dropped to her knees beside Jamison.

"Margaret?" Amber prompted. "Tuck?"

"On my desk," Margaret whispered, as if it was painful for her to talk. "There's a phone list. His cell number is there."

Amber left for Margaret's desk in the outer office.

While she punched Tuck's cell number, the paramedics rushed past with a stretcher. The commotion inside Jamison's office turned into a blur.

"Hello?" Tuck answered.

She cleared her throat, fighting to keep from looking through the office door, afraid of what she might see. She thought she could hear a defibrillator hum to life. Then the paramedics called, "Clear."

"This is Amber Bowen," she said into the phone, struggling to keep her voice from shaking.

There was silence, and she realized Tuck didn't recognize her name. It figured. But this wasn't the time to dwell on his lack of interest in the company that supported his playboy lifestyle.

"I'm Dixon's assistant," she said.

"Oh, Amber. Right." Tuck sounded distracted.

"You need to come to the office." She stopped herself.

What Tuck really needed to do was to go to the hospital and meet the ambulance there. She searched for a way to phrase those words.

"Why?" he asked.

"It's your father."

"My *father* wants me to come to the *office*?" His drawling tone dripped sarcasm.

"We had to call an ambulance."

Tuck's voice became more alert. "Did he fall?"

"He, well, seems to have collapsed."

"*What?* Why?"

"I don't know." She was thinking it had to be a heart attack, but she didn't want to speculate.

"What do you mean you don't know?"

"The paramedics are putting him on a stretcher. I didn't want to call Mrs. Tucker and frighten her."

"Right. Good decision."

"You should probably meet them at Central Hospital."

"Is he conscious?"

Amber looked at Jamison's closed eyes and pale skin. "I don't think so."

"I'm on my way."

"Good."

The line went silent and she set down the phone.

The paramedics wheeled Jamison past. He was propped up on the stretcher, an oxygen mask over his face and an IV in his arm.

Amber sank down onto Margaret's chair, her knees wobbly and her legs weak.

Margaret and the nurse emerged from Jamison's office.

Margaret's eyes were red, tears marring her cheeks.

Amber rose to meet her. "It's going to be all right. He's getting the best of care."

"How?" Margaret asked into the air. "How could this happen?"

The nurse excused herself to follow the paramedics.

"Do you think he has heart problems?" Amber asked quietly.

Margaret shook her head. "He doesn't. Just last night..." Another tear ran down her cheek.

"Did something happen yesterday?" Amber assumed Margaret had meant yesterday, maybe late in the afternoon.

"He was in such a good mood. We had some wine."

"You had wine in the office?"

Margaret stilled. Panic and guilt suddenly flooded her expression, and she took a quick step back, glancing away.

"It was nothing," she said, focusing on some papers in her in-basket, straightening them into a pile.

Amber was stunned.

Jamison and Margaret had been together last night? Had they been *together*, together? It sure looked like it.

Margaret moved briskly around the end of her desk. "I should… That is…" She sank down in her chair.

"Yes," Amber agreed, not sure what she was agreeing to, but quite certain she should end the conversation and get back to her own desk.

She started for the hallway, but then she paused, her sense of duty asserting itself. "I'll call the senior managers and give them the news. Did Jamison tell you about Dixon?"

Margaret looked up. "What about Dixon?"

Amber decided the news of Dixon leaving could wait a couple of hours. "Nothing. We can talk later."

Margaret's head went back down and she plunked a few keys on her keyboard. "Jamison had a lunch today and a three o'clock with the board."

Amber left Margaret to her work, her mind racing with all that would need to be handled.

Dixon was gone. Jamison was ill. And that left no one in charge. Tuck was out there somewhere. But she couldn't even imagine what would happen if Tuck took the reins. He wasn't a real vice president. He was just some partier who dropped by the office now and again, evidently giving heart palpitations to half the female staff.

A week later, Tuck realized he had to accept reality. His father was going to be weeks, if not months, in recovery from his heart attack, and Dixon was nowhere to be found. Somebody had to run Tucker Transportation. And that somebody had to be him.

The senior executives seated around the boardroom table looked decidedly troubled at seeing him in the president's chair. He didn't blame them one bit.

"What I don't understand," said Harvey Miller, the finance director, "is why you're not even talking to Dixon."

Tuck hadn't yet decided how much to reveal about his brother's disappearance. He'd tried calling, text messaging and emailing Dixon. He'd had no response. And there was nothing to go on except the cryptic letter his brother had left for their father, saying he'd be gone a month, maybe even longer.

"Dixon's on vacation," said Tuck.

"Now?" asked Harvey, incredulity ringing through his tone.

Mary Silas's head came up in obvious surprise and chagrin. "I didn't hear about that."

She was in charge of human resources and Tuck knew she prided herself on being in the know.

"Get him back," said Harvey.

Instead of responding to either of them, Tuck scanned the expressions of the five executives. "I'd like a status report from each of you tomorrow morning. Amber will book a one-on-one meeting for each of you."

"What about the New York trade show?" asked Zachary Ingles, the marketing director.

Tuck's understanding of the annual trade show, a marquee event, was sketchy at best. He'd attended a couple of times, so he knew Tucker Transportation created and staffed a large pavilion on the trade-show floor. But in the past he'd been more focused on the booth babes and the evening receptions than on the sales efforts.

"Bring me the information tomorrow," he said.

"I need decisions," said Zachary, his tone impatient.

"Then, I'll make them," Tuck replied.

He might not have a clue what he was doing, but he knew enough to hide his uncertainty.

"Can we at least conference Dixon into the meetings?" asked Harvey.

"He's not available," said Tuck.

"Where is he?"

Tuck set his jaw and glared at the man.

"Do you want a full quarterly report or a summary?" asked Lucas Steele. He was the youngest of the executives, the operations director.

Where the others wore custom-made suits, Lucas was dressed in blue jeans and a dark blazer. His steel-blue shirt was crisp, but he hadn't bothered with a tie. He moved between two worlds—the accountants and lawyers who set strategic direction, and the transport managers around the world who actually got things from A to B.

"A summary is enough for now." Tuck appreciated Lucas's pragmatic approach to the situation.

Lucas raised his brows, silently asking the other men if there was anything else.

Tuck decided to jump on the opportunity and end the meeting.

"Thank you." He rose from his chair.

They followed suit and filed out, leaving him alone with Dixon's assistant, Amber.

He hadn't paid much attention to her before this week, but now she struck him as a model of fortitude and efficiency. Where his father's assistant, Margaret, seemed to be falling apart, Amber was calm and collected.

If she'd wandered out of central casting, she couldn't have looked more perfect for the part of trustworthy assistant. Her brunette hair was pulled back in a tidy French braid. Her makeup was minimal. She wore a gray skirt and blazer with a buttoned white blouse.

Only two things about her tweaked his interest as a man—the fine wisps of hair that had obviously escaped the confining braid, and the spiky black high-heeled sandals that flashed gold soles when she walked. The loose wisps of hair were endearing, while the shoes were intriguing. Both could have the power to turn him on if he was inclined to let them.

He wasn't.

"We need to get Dixon back," he told her, setting his mind firmly on business. His brother was priority number one.

"I don't think we should bother him," she replied.

The answer struck Tuck as ridiculous. "He's got a corporation to run."

Her blue eyes flashed with unexpected annoyance. "*You've* got a corporation to run."

For some reason, he hadn't been prepared for any display of emotion from her, let alone something bordering on hostility. It was yet another thing he found intriguing. It was also something else he was going to ignore.

"We both know that's not going to happen," he stated flatly.

"We both know no such thing."

Tuck wasn't a stickler for hierarchy, but her attitude struck him as inappropriately confrontational. "Do you talk to Dixon this way?"

The question seemed to surprise her, but she recovered quickly. "What way?"

He wasn't buying it. "You know exactly what I mean."

"Dixon needs some time to himself. The divorce was very hard on him."

Tuck knew full well that the divorce had been hard on his brother. "He's better off without her."

"No kidding." There was knowledge in her tone.

"He talked to you about his wife?" Tuck was surprised by that.

Amber didn't reply right away, and it was obvious to him that she was carefully formulating her answer.

He couldn't help wondering how close Dixon had become to his assistant. Was she his confidante? Something more?

"I saw them together," she finally said. "I overheard some of their private conversations."

"You mean you eavesdropped?" Not exactly an admirable trait. Then again, not that he was one to judge.

"I mean, she shouted pretty loud."

"You couldn't leave and give them some privacy?"

"Not always. I have a job that requires me to be at my desk. And that desk is outside Dixon's office."

Tuck couldn't help but wonder exactly how far-reaching her duties had become when Dixon's marriage went bad. He took in her tailored clothes and her neat hair. She might be buttoned down, but she was definitely attractive.

"I see..." He thought maybe he did.

"Stop that," she snapped.

"Stop what?"

"Stop insinuating something without spitting it out. If you've got something to ask me, then *ask* me."

Fine with Tuck. "What were you to my brother?"

She enunciated carefully. "I was his confidential assistant."

He found himself easing forward. "And which of your duties were confidential?"

"All of them."

"You know what I'm asking."

"Then, ask it."

Despite her attitude, he liked her. There was something about her straightforward manner that he admired very much. "Were you sleeping with my brother?"

As he looked into her simmering blue eyes, he suddenly and unexpectedly cared about the answer. He didn't want her to be Dixon's mistress.

"No."

He was relieved. "You're sure?"

"That wouldn't be something I'd forget. My car keys, maybe. To pick up cat food, yes. But, oops, having sex with my boss just slipped my mind?" Her tone went flat. "Yes, Tuck. I'm sure."

He wanted to kiss her. He was suddenly seized by an overwhelming desire to pull her close and taste those sassy lips.

"You have a cat?" he asked instead.

"Focus, Tuck. Dixon's not coming back. At least not for a while. I know you've had a cushy run here, but that's over and done with. You've got work to do now, and I am not letting you duck and weave."

Now he really wanted to kiss her. "How're you going to do that?"

"Persuasion, persistence and coercion."

"You think you can coerce me?"

"What I think is that somewhere deep down inside you must be a man who wants to succeed, a man who actually wants to impress his father."

She was wrong, but he was curious.

"Why do you think that?" he asked.

"You strike me as the type."

"I never imagined I was a type."

Truth was he didn't want to impress his father. But he did want to impress Amber, more than he'd wanted to impress a woman in a very long time.

Unfortunately for him, she wasn't about to observe him in the part of suave, worldly, wealthy Tuck Tucker. She was about to watch him fumbling around the helm of a multimillion corporation. He couldn't have dreamed of a less flattering circumstance.

Two

Amber was torn between annoyance and sympathy.

For the past week, Tuck had arrived at the office promptly at eight. He seemed a little groggy for the first hour, and she'd fallen into the habit of having a large coffee on his desk waiting for him. She could only guess that he hadn't yet modified his playboy nights to fit his workday schedule.

She'd moved from her desk near Dixon's office to the desk outside Tuck's office. Tuck didn't have his own assistant, since he was so rarely there, but now he was taking on Dixon's work. He was also taking on Jamison's. Margaret had been out sick most days since Jamison's heart attack, so Amber was keeping in communication with directors and managers and all of their assistants, trying to be sure nothing fell through the cracks.

This morning, voices were raised behind Tuck's closed door. He was meeting with Zachary Ingles, the marketing director. They were two weeks from the New York trade show and deadlines were rapidly piling up.

"*You* were tasked with approving the final branding," Zachary was shouting. "I sent three options. It's all in the email."

"I have two thousand emails in my in-basket," Tuck returned.

"*Your* disorganization is not *my* problem. We've missed the print deadline on everything—signs, banners and all the swag."

"You need to tell me when there's a critical deadline."

"I did tell you."

"In an email that I didn't read."

"Here's a tip," said Zachary. But then he went silent.

Amber found herself picturing Tuck's glare. Tuck might be out of his depth, but he wasn't stupid, and he wasn't a pushover.

A minute later, Tuck's office door was thrown open and Zachary stormed past her desk, tossing a glare her way. "Tell your boss he can pay rush penalties on every damn item for all I care."

Amber didn't bother to respond. She'd never warmed up to Zachary. He was demanding and entitled, always running roughshod over his staff and anyone else below him in the corporate hierarchy. Dixon put up with him because he was favored by Jamison, and because he did seem to have a knack for knowing how to appeal to big clients with expensive shipping needs.

Tuck appeared in the office doorway.

"Lucas will be here at ten," she told him. "But your schedule is clear for the next half hour."

"Maybe I can read a few hundred emails."

"Good idea."

He drew a breath, looking like he wanted to bolt for the exit. "What am I doing wrong?"

"Nothing."

"I'm behind by two thousand emails."

"Dixon was very organized."

Surely Tuck didn't expect to rival his brother after only a single week. It had taken Dixon years to become such an effective vice president.

Tuck frowned at her. "So everyone tells me."

"He worked very long and hard to get there."

Yes, Tuck was arriving on time. And really, that was more than she'd expected. But Dixon had taken on far more than his fair share of early mornings and late nights working out systems and processes for covering the volume of work. Tuck seemed to expect to become a boy wonder overnight.

Tuck's tone hardened. "I'm asking for some friendly advice. Can we not turn it into a lecture about my sainted brother?"

"You can't expect to simply walk through the door and be perfect."

"I'm not expecting anything of the sort. Believe me, I know that Dixon is remarkable. I've heard about it my entire life."

Amber felt a twinge of guilt.

Tuck did seem to be trying. Not that he had any choice in the matter. And it didn't change the fact that he'd barely bothered to show up at the office until he was backed into a corner. Still, he was here now. She'd give him that.

"Zachary should have given you a heads-up on the branding," she said. "He should have pointed out the deadline."

"I shouldn't have missed it," said Tuck.

"But you did. And you're going to miss other things." She saw no point in pretending.

"Your confidence in me is inspiring."

She found herself annoyed on Tuck's behalf, and the frustration came through in her voice.

"Tell him," she said. "Tell them all. Tell them that it's *their* job to keep you appraised of critical deadlines, and not just in an email. Make it a part of your regular meetings. And make the meetings more frequent if you have to, even daily. I mean, if you can stand to see Zachary every day, that is."

Tuck cracked a smile.

It was a joke. But Amber shouldn't have made it. "I know that was an inappropriate thing to say."

He took a couple of steps toward her desk. "I don't have a problem with inappropriate. It's a good idea. I'll send them an email."

"You don't have to send them an email." Her sense of professionalism won out over her annoyance at his past laziness. "I'll send them an email. And I can triage your in-basket if you'd like."

His expression brightened and he moved closer still. "You'd read them for me?"

"Yes. I'll get rid of the unimportant ones."

"How will you do that?"

"I have a delete key."

He leaned his hands down on the desk, lowering his voice. "You can do that? I mean, and not have the company fall down around my ears?"

Amber found herself fighting a grin. "With some of them, sure. With others, I'll take care of them myself, or I'll delegate the work to one of the unit heads. And I'll flag the important ones for you."

"I swear, I could kiss you for that."

It was obviously a quip. But for some reason his words resonated all the way to her abdomen.

Her gaze went to his lips, triggering the image of a kiss in her imagination.

She caught the look in his eyes and the air seemed to crackle between them.

"Not necessary," she quickly said into the silence.

"I suppose the paycheck is enough."

"It's enough."

He straightened, and a twinkle came into his silver-gray eyes. "Still, the offer's open."

She considered his handsome, unapologetic face and his taut, sexy frame. "You're not like him at all, are you?"

"Dixon?"

She nodded.

"Not a bit."

"He doesn't joke around."

"He should."

Her loyalty reasserted itself. "Are you criticizing Dixon's performance on the job?"

"I'm criticizing his performance in life."

"He's been through a lot."

She didn't know how close Tuck was to his brother, but she had seen firsthand the toll Kassandra's infidelity had taken on Dixon. Dixon had been devoted to his wife. He'd thought they were trying to start a family while she had secretly been taking birth control pills and sleeping with another man.

"I know he has," said Tuck.

"He was blindsided by her lies."

Tuck seemed to consider the statement. "There were signs."

"Now you're criticizing Dixon for loyalty?"

"I'm wondering why you're so blindly defending him."

"When you're an honest person—" as Amber knew Dixon was "—you don't look for deceit in others."

Tuck's gaze was astute. "But you saw it, too."

Amber wasn't going to lie. "That Kassandra had a scheming streak?"

"Aha." There was a distinct ring of triumph in Tuck's tone.

"I saw it, too," she admitted.

He sobered. "I don't know what that says about you and I."

"Maybe that we should be careful around each other?"

"Are you out to get me, Amber?"

"No." She wasn't.

She didn't find him particularly admirable. An admirable man would have shown up to help long before now. But now that he was here, she'd admit he wasn't all bad.

"Are you going to lie to me?"

"No."

"Will you help me succeed?"

She hesitated over that one. "Maybe. If you seem to deserve it."

"How am I doing so far?"

"You're no Dixon."

"I'm never going to be Dixon."

"But you seem to have Zachary's number. I can respect that."

It was a moment before Tuck responded. "How'd he get away with that crap with my dad?"

"He didn't pull that crap with your dad."

"He's testing me."

"We all are."

"Including you?"

"Especially me."

But Tuck was faring better than she'd expected. And she seemed worryingly susceptible to his playboy charm. She was definitely going to have to watch herself around him.

At home in the mansion, Tuck found himself retreating to the second floor, spreading work out in the compact sitting room down the hall from his own bedroom. Stylistically, it was different from the rest of the house, with earth tones, rattan and stoneware accents. He found it restful.

The big house had been built in the early 1900s, with hardwood floors, soaring relief ceilings, elaborate light fixtures and archways twenty feet in height. It was far from the most welcoming place in the world, full of uncomfortable antique chairs and somber paintings. And right now it echoed with emptiness.

Last week, they'd moved his father to a specialized care facility in Boston. His mother had gone with him to stay with her sister. His mother had asked her trusted staff members to come along for what looked to be an extended stay.

Tuck could have replaced the staff. But he was one man, and he had no plans to do any entertaining. Well, maybe a date or two, since he didn't plan to let his responsibilities at Tucker Transportation keep him celibate. But the house still had two cooks, two housekeepers and a groundskeeper. He couldn't imagine needing any more assistance than that.

For now, he headed down the grand staircase to meet his college friend, Jackson Rush, happy with both the opportunity for conversation and the break from office work. While Tuck had studied business at the University of Chicago, Jackson had studied criminology. Jackson now ran an investigations firm that had expanded around the country.

"I hope you have good news," said Tuck as Jackson removed his worn leather jacket and handed it to the housekeeper.

"Dixon took a private jet from Executive Airport to New York City," said Jackson.

"But not a Tucker Transportation jet." Tuck had already checked all the company records.

"Signal Air," said Jackson.

"Because he didn't want my dad to know where he went."

"That seems like a solid theory."

The two men made their way into the sunroom. It was dark outside, not the perfect time to enjoy the view through the floor-to-ceiling windows, but the sunroom was less ostentatious than the library.

"So he's in New York." As far as Tuck was concerned, that was good news. He'd worried his brother had taken off to Europe or Australia.

"From there, it looks like he took a train to Charlotte."

"A train?" Tuck turned his head to frown at Jackson. "Why on earth would he take a train? And what's in Charlotte?"

"Secrecy, I'm guessing." Jackson eased onto a forest-green sofa. "He wouldn't need ID to buy a train ticket. You said your dad tried to stop him from leaving?"

Tuck took a padded Adirondack chair next to a leafy potted ficus. "Dad was terrified at the thought of me actually working at Tucker Transportation."

"Then, I guess things didn't work out so well for him, did they?"

"Are you making a joke about his heart attack?"

"I didn't mean that the way it sounded. From Charlotte, our best guess is Dixon went on to either Miami or New Orleans. Anything you know of for him in either of those cities?"

Tuck racked his brain.

"A woman?" asked Jackson.

"He's barely divorced from Kassandra."

Jackson shot Tuck a look of incredulity.

"She was the one who cheated, not him. I doubt his head was anywhere near to dating again."

"Well, we're checking both cities, but so far he's not using his credit cards or hitting any bank machines. And there's no activity on his cell phone."

Tuck sat back. "Does this strike you as bafflingly elaborate?"

"Your brother does not want to be found. The question is, why?"

"He doesn't know about my dad," said Tuck. "He doesn't know he's abandoned Tucker Transportation to me alone. If he did, he'd be here in a heartbeat."

"Anything else going on in his life? Any chance he's got an enemy, committed a crime, embezzled from the company?"

Tuck laughed at that. "Embezzle from himself? He's got access to all the money he could ever want and then some."

"An enemy, then. Anybody who might want to harm him? Maybe the guy who slept with Kassandra?"

"Dixon's not afraid of Irwin Borba."

"What, then?" asked Jackson.

"He said he needed a vacation."

Tuck wanted to believe that was the simple answer. Because if Dixon was at a beach bar somewhere drinking rum punch and watching women in bikinis, he'd be back home soon. It had already been two weeks. Maybe Tuck just had to hang on a few more days without sinking any ships—either figuratively or literally—and he'd be off the hook. He sure hoped so.

"There's a major trade show coming up in New York," he told Jackson. "And we're launching two new container ships in Antwerp next week. Surely he'll return for that."

"He's expecting your dad will be there." Jackson restlessly tapped his blunt fingers against his denim-covered knee.

That was true. Dixon would assume Jamison would represent the company in Antwerp.

"Have you checked his computer?" asked Jackson. "Maybe he's got a personal email account you don't know about."

"Maybe." Tuck wasn't crazy about the idea of snooping into Dixon's business, but things were getting desperate.

"Check his office computer," said Jackson. "And check his laptop, his tablet, anything he didn't take with him. It looks to me as though he's traveling light."

Tuck had to agree with that. "What's he up to, switching transportation in two different cities?"

"He's up to not being found. And he's doing a damn good job of it. Any chance he's got a secret life?"

"A secret life?"

"Doing things that he can't tell anyone about. He does travel a lot. And he runs in some pretty influential circles."

"Are you asking if my brother is a spy?"

Jackson's shrug said it was possible.

"If there's one thing I've learned in the past week, it's that Dixon couldn't have had time for anything but Tucker Transportation. You wouldn't believe the amount of work that crosses his desk."

"Don't forget you're doing your dad's job, as well," Jackson pointed out.

"Even accounting for that. I'm starting to wonder..."

Tuck wasn't crazy about saying it out loud. But he had to wonder why they hadn't asked for his help before now. Was he truly that inept?

"You're a smart guy, too." Jackson seemed to have guessed the direction of Tuck's thoughts.

"I don't know about that."

"Well, I do. Your dad and Dixon, they probably got into a rhythm together early on. And you never seemed that interested in working at the company."

"I tried." Tuck couldn't keep the defensiveness from his voice. "In the beginning, I tried. But I always seemed to be in the way. Dad definitely didn't want me around. Dixon was his golden boy. After a while you get tired of always barging your way in."

"So you're in it now."

"I am. And it's scaring me half to death."

Jackson grinned. "I've been in the thick of it with you before. I can't picture you being afraid of anything."

"This isn't the same as a physical threat."

"I'm not just talking about a barroom brawl. Remember, I'm running a company of my own."

"That's right." Tuck perked up at the thought of getting some free advice. "You are. How big is it now?"

"Four offices, here in Chicago, New York, Boston and Philly."

"How many employees?"

"About two hundred."

"So you could give me a few tips?"

"Tucker Transportation is on a whole different scale than I am. You're better off talking to your friend Shane Colborn."

"I'm better off finding Dixon."

"I'll fly to Charlotte in the morning."

"You need a jet?"

Jackson cracked a grin. "I'm not going to say no to that offer. Sure, hook me up with a jet. In the meantime, check out his computer."

"I'll get Amber to help."

"Amber?"

"Dixon's trusty assistant."

An image of Amber's pretty face came up in his mind. He wasn't normally a fan of tailored clothes and no-nonsense hairstyles. But she seemed to look good in anything.

And then there were those shoes. She wore a different pair every day, each one sexier than the last. Something was definitely going on beneath the surface there. And the more time he spent with her, the more he wanted to figure out what really made her tick.

When Tuck strode into the office Monday morning, Amber's hormones jumped to attention. He was dressed in a pair of faded jeans, a green cotton shirt and a navy blazer. His dark brown hair had a rakish swoop across the top, and his face had a sexy, cavalier day's growth of beard.

He definitely wasn't Dixon. Dixon's confidence was never

cocky. And Dixon had never made her heart pump faster and heat rise up her neck.

"I need your help," he stated without preamble.

Amber immediately came to her feet. "Is something wrong?"

"Come with me." His walk was decisive and his voice definitive.

She experienced a new and completely inappropriate shiver of reaction.

This was a place of business, she told herself. He wasn't thinking about her as a woman. He sure wasn't thinking the same things she was thinking—that his commanding voice meant he might haul her into his office, pin her up against a wall and kiss her senseless.

What was wrong with her?

Tuck headed into Dixon's office and she forcibly shook off her silly fantasy.

"Do you know his password?" Tuck asked, crossing the big room and rounding the mahogany desk.

"His password to what?" she asked.

"To log on to the system." Tuck leaned down and moved the mouse to bring the screen to life.

She didn't answer. Dixon had given her his password a couple of months back on a day when he was in Europe and needed her to send him some files. She still remembered it, but she knew he'd never intended for her to use it again. What she technically knew, and what she ought to use, were two different things.

Tuck glanced up sharply. "Tell me the password, Amber."

"I..."

"If you don't, I'll only have the systems group reset it."

He made a valid point. As the acting head of Tucker Transportation, he could do whatever he wanted with the company computer system.

"Fine. It's ClownSchool, capital C and S, dollar sign, one, eight, zero."

Tuck typed. "You might want to think about whose side you're on here."

"I'm not taking sides." Though she was committed to keeping her promise to Dixon. "I'm trying to be professional."

"And I'm trying to save Tucker Transportation."

"Save it from what?" Had something happened?

"From ruin without my father or Dixon here to run it."

"What are you looking for?" she asked, realizing that he was exaggerating for effect and deciding to move past the hyperbole.

Tucker Transportation was a solid company with a team of long-term, capable executives running the departments. Even from the top, there was a limited amount of damage anyone could do in a month.

"Clues to where he went," said Tuck.

Then Tuck seemed to have an inspiration. He lifted the desk phone and dialed.

A moment later, a ring chimed inside Dixon's top drawer.

Tuck drew it open and removed Dixon's cell phone, holding it while it rang.

"How does it still have battery power?" he asked, more to himself than anything.

"I've been charging it," said Amber.

His attention switched to her, his face crinkling in obvious annoyance. "You didn't think to *tell me* his cell phone was in his desk drawer?"

Amber wasn't sure how to answer that.

"And how did you know it was there anyway? Were you snooping through his drawers?"

"No." She quickly shook her head. She was intensely respectful of Dixon's privacy. "He told me he was leaving it behind."

Tuck's piercing gray eyes narrowed, his brows slanting together in a way that wrinkled his forehead. "So he told you he was leaving? Before he left, you *knew* he was going?"

Amber realized she'd spoken too fast. But now she had no choice but to give a reluctant nod.

Tuck straightened and came to the end of the desk, his voice gravelly and ominous. "Before you answer this, remember I'm the acting president of this company. This is a direct order, and I don't look kindly on insubordination. Did he tell you where he was going?"

Dixon had given her an emergency number. And she'd recognized the area code. But he hadn't flat-out told her where he was going.

"No," she said, promising herself it wasn't technically a lie. "He needs the time, Tuck. He's been overworked for months, and Kassandra's betrayal hit him hard."

"That's not for you to decide."

She knew that was true. But it wasn't for Tuck to decide, either.

"He doesn't even know about our father," said Tuck.

"If he knew, he'd come home."

Tuck's voice rose. "Of *course* he'd come home."

"And then he'd be back to square one, worse off than he was before. I know it must be hard for you without him."

"You *know*? You don't know anything."

"I've worked here for five years." It was on the tip of her tongue to say that it was a whole lot longer than Tuck had worked here, but she checked herself in time.

"As an *assistant*."

"Yes."

"You don't have the full picture. You don't know the risks, the critical decisions."

"I know Dixon."

Tuck's tone turned incredulous. "You're saying I don't?"

Amber's voice rose. "I'm saying I've been here. I watched how hard he's worked. I saw how much your father slowed down these past months. I watched what Kassandra's infidelity did to him. He was losing it, Tuck. He took a break because he had no other choice."

Tuck gripped the side of the desk, his jaw going tight.

Amber mentally braced herself for an onslaught.

But his voice stayed steady, his words measured. "My father was slowing down?"

"Yes. A lot. Margaret was funneling more and more work to Dixon. Dixon was scrambling. He was staying late, coming in early, traveling all over the world."

"He likes traveling."

"You can't constantly travel and still run a company. And then Kassandra."

"Her behavior was despicable."

"It hurt him, Tuck. Yes, he was disgusted and angry. But he was also very badly hurt."

Tuck rocked back on his heels, his expression going pensive. "He didn't let on."

Amber hesitated but decided to share some more information. If it would help Tuck understand the gravity of the situation, it would do more good than harm.

"There were times when I heard more than I should," she said. "I know Dixon was ready to be a father. He thought they were trying to get pregnant. Instead, she was taking birth control pills and sleeping with another man."

It was clear from Tuck's expression that Dixon hadn't shared that information with him. He sat down, and his gaze went to the computer screen. "He still needs to know about our father."

She knew it wasn't her place to stop Tuck. "Do what you need to do."

He glanced up. "But you're not going to help me?"

"There's nothing more I can do to help you find Dixon. But I'll help you run Tucker Transportation."

"Finding Dixon is the best thing we can do to run Tucker Transportation."

"I disagree," she said.

"Bully for you."

"The best thing you can do to run Tucker Transportation is to *run* Tucker Transportation."

Tuck was silent while he moved the mouse and typed a few keys. "You should have told me."

"Told you what?" She found herself moving around the desk, curious to see what he would find on the computer.

"What he was planning," said Tuck as he scrolled through Dixon's email. "That he was secretly leaving."

She recognized the headers on the email messages, since they automatically copied to her account. "I'm Dixon's confidential assistant. I don't share his personal information with anyone else."

"There's nothing here but corporate business," said Tuck.

Amber knew that would be the case. Dixon was always careful to keep his personal email out of the corporate system. And he'd been doubly careful with the details of his secret vacation.

Tuck swiveled the chair to face her. "What would you do if you were mine?"

The question caught her off guard while her brain zipped off on a disorienting, romantic tangent. To be Tuck's. In his arms. In his life. In his bed.

He rose in front of her. "Amber?"

"Sorry?" She scrambled to bring her thoughts back to the real world.

His voice was rich and deep, laced with an intimacy she knew she had to be imagining. "If you were *my* confidential assistant, what would you do?"

"I'm not." She wasn't his anything, and she had to remember that.

"But if you were?"

If she was Tuck's assistant, she'd be in the middle of making one colossal mistake. Because that would mean she was sexually attracted to her boss. She'd want to kiss her boss. Eventually, she *would* kiss her boss. She was thinking about it right now. And if the dusky smoke in his eyes was anything to go by, he was thinking about it, too.

She plunged right in with the truth. "I would probably make a huge and horrible mistake."

The lift of his brows told her he understood her meaning. And he slowly raised his hand to brush his fingertips across her cheek. "Would it be so horrible?"

"We can't," she managed to respond.

He gave a very small smile. "We won't."

But he was easing closer, leaning in.

"Tuck," she warned.

He used his other hand to take hold of hers, twining their fingers together. "Professionally. On a professional level, given the current circumstances, what would you do if your loyalty was to me?"

She called on every single ounce of her fortitude to focus. "I'd tell you to go to the New York trade show. It's the smart thing to do and the best thing to do for the company."

"Okay."

His easy answer took her aback.

She wasn't sure she'd understood correctly. "You'll go?"

"We'll both go. I'm still going to find Dixon. But until I do, I'm the only owner this company has got. You're right to tell me to step up."

Amber moved a pace back and he released her hand.

New York? Together? With Tuck?

She struggled for a way to state her position. "I don't want you to get the wrong idea. I'm definitely not going to—"

"Sleep with me?" he said, finishing her thought.

"Well. Okay. Yes. That's what I meant." She hadn't planned on being that blunt, but that was it.

"That's disappointing. But it's not the reason I want you in New York. And I promise, there'll be no pressure on that front." He smoothly closed the space between them and leaned down.

She waited, her senses on alert for the kiss that seemed inevitable.

But he stopped, his lips inches away from hers, his voice a whisper. "I really like your shoes."

She reflexively glanced to her feet, seeing the jazzy, swirling gold-and-red pattern of her high-heel pumps.

"They'll look good in New York." He backed off, his voice returning to normal as he took his place in front of the computer screen. "Let's stay at the Neapolitan. Book us on a flight."

Once again, she fought to regain her emotional equilibrium. She swallowed. "Do you want an airline ticket or should I book a company plane?"

"What would Dixon do?"

"Dixon never flies commercial."

Tuck grinned. "Then, book us a company plane. If I'm going to take Dixon's place, I might as well enjoy all his perks."

Amber wanted to ask if he considered her one of Dixon's perks. But the question was as inappropriate as it was dangerous. Her relationship with Dixon was comfortably professional. By contrast, her relationship with Tuck grew more unsettling by the day.

Three

Tuck knew he had no right to be cheerful. Dixon was still missing and Zachary Ingles was unforgivably late arriving at the JWQ Convention Center in midtown Manhattan. Add to that, thirty Tucker Transportation employees were working with the convention center staff to assemble the components of the company's pavilion, with less organization than he would have expected.

Still he couldn't help but smile as he gazed across the chaos of lights, signs, scale models and scaffolding. Amber was at the opposite end of their allotted space, watching a forklift raise the main corporate sign into position. Her brunette hair was in a jaunty ponytail. She wore pink-and-black checkerboard sneakers, a pair of dark blue jeans and a dusky-blue pullover. It was as casual as he'd ever seen her.

"Mr. Tucker?" A woman in a navy blazer with a convention center name tag on the lapel approached him through the jumble. "I'm Nancy Raines, assistant manager with catering and logistics."

Tuck offered his hand. "Nice to meet you, Nancy. Please call me Tuck."

"Thank you, sir." She referred to the tablet in her hand. "We have the east-side ballroom booked for Friday night, a customized appetizers and hors d'oeuvres menu with an open bar for six hundred."

"That sounds right," said Tuck.

He'd read through the company's final schedule on the plane and he understood the general outline of each event. Out of the corner of his eye, he saw Amber coming their way.

"We understand that there was a last-minute booking of a

jazz trio, Three-Dimensional Moon," said Nancy. "Are they by any chance an acoustic band?"

"An acoustic band for six hundred people?" Tuck found the question rather absurd. How would anyone ever hear the music above the conversation?

"The reason I ask," said Nancy, "is we have no arrangement in place for a sound system."

"There's no sound system?"

That was clearly a mistake. Aside from the music, there were three speeches on the event schedule and a ten-minute corporate video.

Amber arrived. "Can I help with something?"

"This is Nancy. She says there's no sound system for the reception."

"There should be a sound system," said Amber. "And three projection screens."

But Nancy was shaking her head. "There was no tech ordered at all."

"Someone from the marketing department should have handled that. Have you heard anything from Zachary?" Tuck asked Amber. He needed to get to the bottom of this right away.

"I've texted, emailed and left a voice mail, but he's not returning."

Tuck withdrew his phone from his pocket. "We'll need the tech setup," he said to Nancy. "Can you take care of it?"

She made a few taps on her tablet. "I can try. It will have to be rush, and that'll mean a significant surcharge." She looked to Amber. "Do you have the specs?"

"I'll get them to you," said Amber, pulling out her own phone. "I'll track someone down."

Nancy handed her a business card. "You can send them to my email. I'll call a couple of local companies."

"Thanks," said Amber.

Tuck pressed the speed dial for Zachary.

Once again, it rang through to his voice mail.

"Maybe his flight was delayed," Tuck mused.

Amber held up her index finger. “Melanie? It’s Amber. We need specs for a sound system for Three-Dimensional Moon. Can you find their web page and contact their manager?” She paused. “In the next ten minutes if you can.”

Tuck checked his text messages, and then he moved to his email interface.

“I’ve got a new message from Zachary.” He tapped the header.

He read for a minute and felt his jaw go lax.

“What?” Amber asked.

“It’s a letter of resignation.”

“No way.” She moved to where she could see his small screen.

“It says he turned in his keys to security and asked them to change his password.”

Tuck had no idea what to make of the message. Zachary had been with the company for a decade, rising through the ranks to his current, very well-paid position.

“Why would he do that?”

Excellent question.

Tuck’s phone rang. He saw that it was Lucas Steele.

Tuck took the call, speaking without preamble. “Do you know what’s going on?”

“Zachary walked,” said Lucas.

“I just got his email. Do you know why?”

“Harvey went with him,” said Lucas.

“Harvey, too? What on earth *happened*?” Tuck couldn’t keep the astonishment from his voice. Two long-term directors had quit at the same time?

Amber’s eyes widened while she listened to his side of the conversation.

“Peak Overland made them an offer,” said Lucas.

“Both of them?”

“Yes.”

The situation came clear in Tuck’s mind. “Without Dixon, we look vulnerable.”

"Yes, we look vulnerable. Nobody knows anything concrete, so there are theories all over the place. I'm hearing everything from he's been thrown in jail in a foreign country to he was killed skydiving."

"He's in New Orleans," said Tuck. "Or maybe Miami."

There was a silence.

"You don't know where he is." Lucas's voice was flat.

"He's on vacation. He needs some time alone."

"The divorce?" asked Lucas.

"That's my best guess."

"Okay," said Lucas, his tone growing crisp again. "You need me to come out there?"

"Yes. But I also need you in Chicago. And I need you in Antwerp."

What Tuck really needed was Dixon and there was absolutely no time to waste. His next call would be to Jackson.

Lucas gave a chopped chuckle. "Where do you want me?"

"Can you hold the fort in Chicago?"

"I can."

"Talk to security. Change the locks, change the system passwords. Make sure they can't do any damage."

"Will do."

"Is there an heir apparent to either Zachary or Harvey?"

"Nobody comes instantly to mind. But I'll think about it. And I'll ask around."

"Thanks. Talk to you in a few hours."

Tuck's lack of knowledge and experience with the family company suddenly felt like an anvil. He needed his brother more urgently than ever before.

"I'd choose Hope Quigley," said Amber.

"Who?"

"She's a manager in the marketing department. She's been on the social media file for a couple of years, but she's incredibly organized."

"You want me to promote a blogger to marketing director?"

Amber frowned. "It's a lot more than just blogging."

"That's a huge jump in responsibility."

Her hand went to her hip. "And you'd know this, how?"

Tuck did not want to have to make this decision on his own. "I'm calling Jackson. No more messing around. We're turning over every possible rock to find Dixon."

Something shifted in Amber's expression. "You don't need Dixon back."

What an absurd statement. "I absolutely need Dixon back."

"You can promote Hope. And there are others who can step in."

"The company needs a strong president. Look around you. We've got two days to pull this thing together. The reception is already in trouble, and there are thirty private meetings set up with the *marketing director*."

"You take the meetings."

"Yeah, right." As if he was going to speak knowledgably about Baltic Exchange indices and intermodal freight transport.

"Take Hope with you. Give her a new title. She's got two days before the meetings. She can come up to speed on the specific client accounts."

"I've never ever met the woman."

"Then, take Lucas with you."

"Lucas has to keep our current freight moving across the ocean."

"You're right." Amber pursed her red lips, folding her hands primly in front of her. "It's all hopeless. We should just give up and go home."

He didn't have a comeback for her obvious sarcasm. He knew what she was doing, and he didn't appreciate it.

"Are you this insubordinate with Dixon?" How had she kept from being fired?

Tuck dialed Jackson.

"I don't need to be insubordinate with Dixon. He knows what he's doing."

"Well, I..." But there was no retort for that. Tuck didn't know what he was doing. And that was the problem.

Jackson answered his phone. "Hi, Tuck."

"You need to pull out the stops," said Tuck. "Do whatever it takes."

"But—" Amber began.

Tuck silenced her with a glare. "I just lost my marketing director and my finance director."

"Did you fire them?" asked Jackson.

"They quit. Rumor has it they got an offer from a rival, and with Dixon out of the picture—"

"People are getting nervous." Jackson filled in the thought.

"It seems I'm not seen as a strong leader."

"You've barely gotten started."

Tuck knew that was no excuse. Maybe he should have barreled past his father's objections years ago. They might have been able to stop him from having any power at Tucker Transportation. But they couldn't have stopped him from learning. This was his fault, and he had to fix it.

"Find him," he said to Jackson.

"I'm in New Orleans."

"Do you think he's there?"

"I don't know that he's not. There's no evidence that he left."

"Is there evidence he arrived?"

"Maybe. It could be nothing. Can I get back to you?"

"Don't take too long." Tuck's gaze met Amber's.

She gave a slight shake of her head.

He knew she wanted him to leave Dixon alone and do it all himself. But there was too much at stake. He didn't dare try.

Tuck looked fantastic in a tuxedo. But then Amber had known that all along. She'd been seeing pictures of him in the tabloids for years, mostly at posh events or out on the town with some gorgeous woman. His ability to work a party had never been in question.

The Tucker Transportation reception was ending, and the

last few guests trickled out of the ballroom. Amber made her way to the main doors, grateful to have the evening at an end. Her feet were killing her, though that was her own fault. She'd knowingly worn two-hour shoes to a five-hour party.

But she hadn't been able to resist. This was by far the fanciest party she'd ever attended. And she'd never even taken the silver lace peep-toe pumps out of the box. They had a crimson stiletto heel and she'd done her toenails to match. Her feet looked fabulous, setting off her rather simple black dress.

The dress had cap sleeves and a slim silhouette. Its one jazzy feature was the scattering of silver sequins at the midthigh hemline. She'd worn it at least a dozen times, but it was tried and true, appropriate to the occasion.

Tuck appeared beside her, lightly touching her waist. "You promised me a dance."

"Your dance card seemed full," she answered him.

"Women kept asking, and I didn't want to be rude."

Amber kept walking toward the elevator. "You forget the point of hosting such a lavish reception was for you to make business contacts, not to collect phone numbers."

"You sound jealous."

She wasn't jealous. She refused to be jealous. She was merely feeling critical of his wasted opportunities.

"That was a business observation, not a personal one."

"No?" he asked.

"No."

Though, at the moment, it felt intensely personal. His hand was still resting at her waist. The heat from his body called out to her. And his deep voice seemed to seep through to her bones.

"Dance with me now."

She steeled herself against the attraction. "The band is packing up."

The only music was the elevator kind emanating from the small hotel speakers on the ceiling.

"We can go somewhere else."

"It's late. My feet are killing me. And I don't know why I'm giving you excuses. No. I don't want to go somewhere else and dance with you. I want to go to bed."

He let a beat go by in silence. Then there was a lilt in his voice. "Okay. Sure. That works for me."

They came to the elevators. "Tell me you didn't mean that how it sounded."

He pressed the call button. "That depends. How did it sound?"

"You can't flirt with me, Tuck."

"Am I doing it wrong?"

"That's not what I—"

"It was a great party, Amber. Against all odds, we got our pavilion up and running in time. The crowds have been super. And the party came off without a hitch. We even had a good sound system. Thank you for that, by the way. Can we not let our guard down and enjoy the achievement for just a few minutes?"

"I work for you."

She needed to nip his playboy behavior in the bud. It didn't matter that he was a charming flirt. And it didn't matter that he was sharp and funny and killer handsome. This wasn't a date. It was a corporate function, and she wasn't going to let either of them forget it.

"So what?" His question seemed sincere.

"So you can't hit on me."

"Is that a rule?"

"Yes, it's a rule. It's a law. It's called sexual harassment."

"I'm not seriously asking you to sleep with me. I mean, I wouldn't say no to an offer, obviously. But I'm not making the suggestion myself. Except, well, you know, in the most oblique and joking way possible."

Amber was stupefied. She had no idea what to say.

The elevator door opened, but neither of them moved.

"You're my boss," she tried.

"Dixon is your boss."

"You know what I mean."

"Are you saying I can't even ask you on a date? That's ridiculous. People date their bosses all the time. Some of them marry their bosses, for goodness' sake."

The door slid closed again.

She couldn't seem to stop herself from joking. "Are we getting married, Tuck?"

He didn't miss a beat. "I don't know. We haven't even had our first date."

She blew out a sigh of frustration. "What I'm saying, what the law says, is that you can't in any way, shape or form hint that my agreement or lack of agreement to something sexual or romantic will impact my job."

"I'm not doing that. I'd never do that. How do I prove it? Is there something I can sign?"

She pressed the call button again. "Tuck, you have got to spend more time in the real world."

"I spend all my time in the real world."

The door slid back open and they walked inside the elevator.

She turned to face the front. "If you did, you'd know what I was talking about."

"I do know what you're talking about. All I wanted to do was dance."

The door slid shut and they were alone in the car.

He was right. She didn't know how the conversation had gotten so far off track.

"We don't have time to dance," she told him. "You need to focus on tomorrow's meetings. You have the list, right? Did you study the files?"

"I looked at them."

"What does that mean?"

"I scanned them. I know the basics. Besides, you agreed to be there with me."

"You can't defer to your assistant when you're meeting with owners and executives of billion-dollar companies."

"I've been busy. I had to work some things out with Lucas. And then I took your advice and interviewed Hope."

"You did?" Amber was glad to hear that.

"Yes. I liked her. I'm going to give her more responsibility."

"That's good."

"So forgive me if I didn't find time to memorize the details of thirty client files."

Amber was tired, but she shook her brain back to life. Thank goodness she'd said no to the second glass of champagne.

"We'll go over them tonight," she told him.

He glanced at his watch.

"Unless you want to get up at 4:00 a.m. and go over them in the morning."

"Four a.m. is a late night, not an early morning."

"You're starting with a breakfast meeting."

"I know. Who set that up? Breakfast meetings are evil. They should be banned."

The elevator came to a stop on the top floor.

"Let's get this over with," Amber said with resignation.

Together, they walked the length of the hall to Tuck's suite. She'd been in it yesterday, so she knew it wasn't a typically intimate hotel room.

The main floor was a living area, powder room and kitchenette. You had to climb a spiral staircase to even get to the bedroom. According to the floor plan sketched on the door, there was a whirlpool tub on the bedroom terrace, but she had no intention of finding out in person.

As she set her clutch purse down on a glass-topped table and slipped off her shoes, her phone chimed. Curious as to who would text her at such a late hour, she checked the screen.

She was surprised to see it was her sister.

Jade lived on the West Coast and only contacted Amber if she needed money or was having an emotional crisis. It was uncharitable, and maybe unfair, but Amber's first thought was that Jade might be in jail.

"Are you thirsty?" Tuck asked, crossing to the bar.

Amber sat down on a peach-colored sofa. It was arranged in a grouping with two cream-colored armchairs in front of a marble fireplace.

"Some water would be nice," said Amber, opening the text message.

"Water? That's it?"

"I'd take some fruit juice."

I just hit town, Jade's text said.

"You're a wild woman," said Tuck.

"I'm keeping my wits about me."

Which town? Amber answered her sister.

"In case I make a pass at you?" asked Tuck.

"You swore you wouldn't."

"I don't recall signing anything."

Chicago.

What's wrong? Amber typed to her sister.

Nothing all good. Well, dumped boyfriend. Jerk anyway.

"Amber?" Tuck prompted.

"Hmm?"

"I said I didn't sign anything."

She glanced up. "Anything for what?"

He nodded to her phone. "Who's that?"

"My sister."

"You checked out there. I thought it might be your boyfriend."

"I don't have a boyfriend." She absently wondered what she'd ever said or done to make Tuck believe she had a boyfriend.

I'm in New York City, Amber typed to Jade.

"Good," said Tuck in a soft tone.

A shimmer tightened her chest.

I was hoping to crash with you for a couple of days, Jade responded.

Amber's fingers froze and she stared at the screen.

"What does she say?" asked Tuck, moving closer.

"She wants to stay with me."

"Is that bad?"

"She's not particularly…trustworthy."

Jade was constantly in and out of low-paying jobs, and in and out of bad relationships. The last time she'd stayed with Amber her sister had prompted a noise complaint from a neighbor, drunk all of Amber's wine and left abruptly without a goodbye, taking two pairs of Amber's jeans and several of her blouses along for good measure.

I'll call you when I get back, Amber typed.

"Oh?" Tuck took a seat on the other end of the sofa.

Thing is, Jade returned, I kind of need a place now, tonight.

Amber swore under her breath. It was coming up on midnight in Chicago, and her little sister had nowhere to go. She didn't delude herself that Jade would have money for a hotel.

"What is it?" asked Tuck.

"She needs a place now."

"Right now?" He glanced at his watch.

"I'm guessing she just got in from LA." Amber wouldn't be surprised if Jade had hitchhiked.

Hotel? Amber wrote.

Can't afford it. Jerk took all the money.

Of course the jerk boyfriend took Jade's money. They always did.

"I take it cash flow is an issue," said Tuck.

"That's a polite way to put it."

"Send her to the nearest Aquamarine location."

Amber raised her brow in Tuck's direction. The Aquamarine was a quality, four-star hotel chain.

"Tucker Transportation has a corporate account," said Tuck.

"I know Tucker Transportation has a corporate account."

"You can tell her to use it."

"I can't misuse the company account for my sister."

"You can't," he agreed. "But I can."

"I won't—"

"I need your attention," said Tuck. "I need you off your cell phone and I need you not worrying about your sister. The way I see it, this is the cheapest way forward."

"That's a stretch."

Tuck's tone turned serious. "Tell her. Let me make that an order."

Amber wanted to argue. But then she didn't particularly want to send Jade to her town house, nor did she want to rouse a neighbor at this hour to give her a key.

"I know you respect orders," said Tuck. "You are the consummate professional."

"You're messing in my personal life." Amber knew she shouldn't take him up on it, but she was sorely tempted.

"Yeah," he said. "I am. Now send her to the Aquamarine."

Amber heaved a sigh.

Before she could send the message, Tuck scooped the phone out of her hand, typing into it.

"Hey!"

"You know it's the best answer."

She did know it was the best answer. And she'd been about to do it herself. Further protests seemed pointless.

"She says great," said Tuck.

"I'll bet she does."

He set the phone down on the coffee table. "You're a good sister."

"In this instance, I think you're the good sister."

"Never been called that before."

"Neither have I."

Tuck chuckled, obviously assuming she was making a joke.

She wasn't.

Four

Tuck was pretty good at handling late nights, but even he was starting to fade by the time he and Amber shut down the last client file. She looked exhausted, her cheeks flushed, makeup smudged under her eyes and her hair escaping in wisps from the updo.

"That's as ready as we can be," she said.

They were side by side on the overstuffed sofa, a lamp glowing on an end table, the lights of the city streaming through open curtains on the picture window across the room.

Tuck had long since shrugged out of his suit jacket and loosened his tie. His shirtsleeves were rolled up, but he was still too warm. The thermostat might be set too high. More likely, it was his attraction to Amber.

She was intensely sexy, every single thing about her, from her deep blue eyes to her rich brunette hair, to the delicious, sleek curves revealed by her fitted dress.

"Do you feel confident?" she asked, tipping her head to look at him.

He realized he'd been silently staring at her.

And he was still staring at her. He was overwhelmed by the urge to kiss her, kiss her deeply and thoroughly, taste those soft, dark red lips that had been teasing his senses all night long. He knew he shouldn't. Her earlier reluctance was reasonable and well founded. Anything romantic between them was bound to be complicated, today, tomorrow and into the future.

"Tuck?" she persisted, clearly confused.

He lifted his hand, brushed the stray hairs back from her cheek.

She sucked in a quick breath and her eyes closed in a long

blink. When they opened, they were opaque, misty blue with indecision.

It wasn't a no, he told himself. She wasn't ordering him to back off. She was tempted, just like him.

He knew there had to be a whole lot of reasons not to do this, but he couldn't seem to come up with them at the moment. So he leaned forward instead, slowly and steadily.

She could stop him, run away from him, pull back from him at least. Whatever she decided, he'd accept. But he had to at least try.

She didn't do any of those things, and their lips came together, his bold and purposeful, hers heated, smooth and delicious. He altered the angle and his arms went around her. He kissed her once, twice, three times, desire pulsing through his mind and electrifying his body.

She kissed him back, tentatively at first. But then her tongue touched his, tangled with his. Her body went malleable against his, her softness forming to his planes. He eased her back on the sofa, covering her from chest to thighs, tasting her mouth, inhaling her scent, feeling her back arch intimately and her heartbeat rise against his chest.

He wanted her bad.

He kissed his way down her neck, pushing the cap sleeve of her dress out of the way, leaving damp circles on her bare shoulder. He thought about her zipper, imagined pulling it down her back, the dress falling away, revealing a lacy bra, or her bare breasts, that creamy smooth skin that was silken to his touch.

"Tuck?" Her voice was breathless.

"Yes?"

"We…"

He stilled. He knew what came next, though every fiber of his being rebelled against it.

"Can't," she said, finishing the thought.

He wanted to argue. They could. They really could, and the world wouldn't come to a crashing halt.

But he'd never coerced a woman into his bed before and he wasn't about to start with Amber.

"You sure?" he asked.

He could feel her nod.

"I'm sorry," she said.

He eased back. "No, I'm the one who's sorry. I shouldn't have kissed you."

"I should have said no."

"I'm glad you didn't."

"I'm… Oh, this is not good." She struggled to sit up.

He moved out of the way, offering his hand to help her up.

Neither of them seemed to know what to say.

Tuck broke the silence. "I guess we're ready for the meeting."

"Tuck, I—"

"You don't have to explain."

A woman was entitled to say no for any reason she wanted. And he did understand her hesitation. She worked for him, at least temporarily. She was smart not to let it get complicated.

She rose to her feet. "You're an attractive guy. But you know that."

He stood.

"I'm sure most women would—"

"I don't like where this is going." He didn't.

"I know you don't often get turned down."

"Now, how would you know that?"

"I read the papers."

His annoyance grew. "You believe the tabloids?"

"They have pictures." Frustration crept into her tone. "You can't deny you have gorgeous girl after gorgeous girl on your arm."

"Is that what you think of me? I didn't kiss you because you're beautiful, Amber."

"I *know* that. I'm not comparing myself to them."

"Comparing yourself?" He didn't understand her point.

"I'm not suggesting I'm one of your bombshells."

"Good."

She was so much more than that. He might not have known her long, but he knew there was more depth to her than a dozen of his Saturday-night dates combined.

Her shoulders dropped. "I'll just say good night."

"You didn't do anything wrong."

He didn't want her to leave. He wanted to keep talking, even if they were arguing. He liked the sound of her voice. But he also wanted to kiss her again and carry her off to his bed. He couldn't do that.

"It's late," she said. "We're both tired. Let's not say or do anything we're going to regret."

"I don't regret a thing."

"I do."

The words were like a blow to his chest. "I'm sorry to hear that."

"I'm your employee, Tuck."

"You're Dixon's employee."

"Tucker Transportation's employee. And you're a vice president."

"In name only." He found himself parroting his father's words.

"You need to change that, Tuck. You really do."

"Are you lecturing me on my corporate responsibility?"

"Somebody has to."

He was about to retort that they already had. But then he realized it wasn't true. Neither his father nor Dixon had lectured him. They'd never pushed him to become more involved in the company. They'd barely suggested he show up. But he wasn't about to admit that to Amber.

He had to stop himself from taking her hands in his. "How did we get here?"

Her eyes narrowed in puzzlement. "We were prepping for the client meetings."

"I meant in the conversation. We were talking about us, and suddenly we're on to Tucker Transportation."

"There is no us."

"There was almost an us."

It was barely there, but he could tell she stifled a smile. It warmed his heart.

"I'm leaving now," she said.

He reflexively grasped her hands. "You don't have to go."

"I do have to go."

"Stay." He gave himself a mental shake, backing off. "I'm sorry. I never do that. I never try to convince a woman to sleep with me."

She arched a brow. "They normally throw themselves into your bed?"

They did. But he knew how that sounded.

"I like you, Amber."

"I'm not going to sleep with you, Tuck."

"That's not what I'm asking."

"It's exactly what you're asking. It's 2:00 a.m., and I'm in your hotel room." She hesitated. "That was my mistake, wasn't it? What was I thinking?"

"You didn't make a mistake."

She tugged her hands from his. "I didn't think this through. I just assumed you wouldn't misunderstand."

"I didn't misunderstand. I didn't plan this, Amber." He'd taken her behavior at face value. He knew she was only trying to help him get ready for the meetings.

She held up her palms and took a couple of backward paces. "Time for me to say good night. Don't forget the breakfast meeting." She took her purse from the table. "Don't be late."

"I'm never late."

"True," she allowed as she retrieved her shoes and strode toward the door. "But I always expect you to be late."

"Why?"

"I'll see you tomorrow." And then she was gone.

He wanted to call her back. He *wished* he could call her back. But he'd made enough mistakes for one night. He realized that if he wanted Amber to let him get anywhere close to her, he had to back off until she was ready.

Back in Chicago two days later, Amber dreaded meeting up with Jade. She was happy her sister had dumped whatever loser boyfriend she'd hooked up with this time, but she also held out no hope for the next one, or the one after that. Bad boyfriends and heartache had been Jade's pattern since she'd dropped out of high school.

Amber tried to harden her heart. Jade was an adult and responsible for her own behavior. But Amber couldn't help remembering her sister as a lost little girl, younger, who had struggled even more than Amber with their mother's addiction to alcohol.

She made her way from her car up the stone pathway to the lobby of the Riverside Aquamarine. Jade was going to meet her in the coffee shop. But since it was shortly after noon, Amber wasn't going to be surprised to find her in the lobby lounge. It was sadly ironic that Jade had turned to alcohol to combat a childhood ruined by alcohol.

The hotel lobby was bright and airy, decorated by white armchairs and leafy plants. The lobby lounge was central, but Amber didn't see Jade at any of the tables. She moved on to the coffee shop that overlooked the pool and quickly spotted Jade at a booth.

As Amber approached, Jade slid from the bench and came to her feet.

Amber's jaw nearly dropped to the floor.

Jade was pregnant. She was very, very pregnant.

"What on earth?" Amber paced forward, coming to a stop in front of her sister.

"Seven months," said Jade, giving a wry smile as she answered the obvious question.

"But…when? How?"

Jade's expression sobered. "Seven months ago. And the usual way. Can we sit down?"

"Oh, Jade." Amber couldn't keep the disappointment and worry from her tone. Jade was in no position to be a good mother.

"Don't 'oh, Jade' me. I'm happy."

"How can you be happy?"

"I'm going to be a mother." Jade slid back into the booth.

As she took the seat across from her, Amber noted she was eating a salad and drinking a glass of iced tea. "You're not drinking, are you?"

"It's iced tea," said Jade.

"I don't mean now. I mean *at all*. You can't drink while you're pregnant, Jade."

"Do you think I'm stupid?"

Stupid, no. But Jade's judgment had always been a big question mark.

"That's not an answer," Amber pointed out.

"No, I'm not drinking."

"Good. That's good. You've seen a doctor?"

"Yes, I saw a doctor in LA. And I'll find a clinic here in Chicago, too."

A waitress appeared and Amber ordered a soda.

She stared at her sister, noting the worn cotton smock and the wrinkled slacks. Jade's cheeks looked hollow and her arms looked thin. Amber hated to think her sister might not be getting enough to eat.

All the way here, she'd been hoping Jade's stay in Chicago would be brief. She'd dreaded the idea of having her move into the town house for days or weeks. Now she realized that was exactly what had to happen. Jade needed stability, a warm bed, good food.

"Have you been taking care of yourself?" Amber asked.

Jade gave a shrug. "It's been okay. Kirk was getting more and more obnoxious about the baby. He said he didn't mind, but then he started talking about putting it up for adoption."

Amber's opinion of this Kirk person went up a notch. "*Have* you thought about adoption?"

Jade's expression twisted in anger. "I am *not* giving away this baby."

"To a good home," said Amber. "There are fantastic prospective parents out there. Loving, well educated, houses in the suburbs—they could give a baby a great life."

Jade's lips pressed together and her arms crossed protectively over her stomach. "Forget it."

"Okay," said Amber, letting the subject drop for now. "It's your choice."

"Damn right it's my choice."

"Yours and the father's."

"There is no father."

"You just said Kirk wanted to give the baby up for adoption."

"Kirk's not the father. That's why he wanted to give the baby away. It's not his."

The revelation took Amber aback. Kirk dropped back down in her esteem. "I don't understand."

"I was pregnant when I met Kirk. He said he didn't mind. He said he loved kids. But then…" Jade gave another shrug.

"Who's the father?" asked Amber. Maybe there was some hope for financial support. Heaven knew Jade was going to need it.

"It was a one-night thing."

"You didn't get his name." Amber shouldn't have been surprised.

"Only his first name. Pete."

Amber tried not to judge, but it was hard.

"He was a sailor."

"You mean in the navy?"

Jade nodded.

"Well, did you try to find him?"

"It was weeks before I knew I was pregnant."

"What about DNA? After the baby's born. The navy must have a database."

"He was Australian."

"Still, did you contact—"

"Amber, I am not going to track down some Australian sailor and ruin his life over a one-night stand."

"Why not? He ruined—"

"Don't you *dare* say he ruined mine. He seemed like a really nice guy. But I went into it with my eyes wide-open, and it was my choice to carry on with the pregnancy. I'm having a baby, my son or daughter, your nephew or niece, and I'm going to take care of it, and I'm not going to drag some poor man kicking and screaming into an obligation he didn't sign up for."

Jade's words and attitude were surprising but in some ways admirable. Amber wasn't used to her taking such personal responsibility.

"Okay," she told her sister. "You can come and stay with me."

Jade was silent for a moment. "Thank you."

"We'll figure this out together."

But Jade was shaking her head. "I'm not looking for you to take over my life."

Who'd said anything about taking over?

"It's only temporary," Jade continued. "I'm studying. I'm going to write my GED. Then I'm going to get a proper job."

Amber could barely believe what she was hearing. "You're working on your GED?"

"I've been working on it for months now."

The surprises just kept on coming. "Seriously?"

"Why would I joke about that?"

"That's fantastic." Amber was beyond impressed. "I'll help you. We can—"

"Whoa. You need to dial it down."

"I didn't mean to dial it up."

"Giving me a place to stay is great, *really* great. But that's all I need right now."

Amber forcibly curbed her excitement. But it was the first time Jade had shown an interest in anything but partying, and Amber's hopes were running away with her. A baby was an enormous responsibility. But other single mothers had pulled it off. If Jade could keep up this new attitude, she might have a fighting chance.

Amber couldn't help but smile at the possibilities, even as Jade came back with a warning frown.

"I thought we'd have him back by now," Tuck said to Jackson.

It was late-afternoon Tuesday, a week after the New York trip, and the rain was streaming in sheets down the picture window overlooking the river. The two men lounged in the armchair group in the corner of Tuck's office. Tuck's desk was piled with paper and his email in-box was approaching the breaking point. Most of it was bad news, and he was anxious for Dixon's return.

"I thought so, too," said Jackson. He had one ankle over the opposite knee, his legs clad in black jeans topped with a steel-gray T-shirt. "Your brother's wreaking havoc with my reputation."

"I know I'm losing faith in you," said Tuck. "And I'm beginning to consider the wild rumors."

"That he's a spy?"

"That there's at least something going on that I don't know about." Tuck didn't believe Dixon had a secret life. But he was all out of reasonable explanations. It had been nearly a month since his brother had disappeared.

"Is there anything we could have missed?" asked Jackson. "Some paper record, a secret email account, a different cell phone?"

"I've searched his office. I've looked through the mansion. I even called Kassandra."

"You *called* Kassandra?"

"You didn't?"

"Of course I did. But it's my job to chase down every lead."

"It's my company," said Tuck. "And it's going rapidly downhill without Dixon."

"What was your take on Kassandra?" asked Jackson.

"That's she's a selfish, spoiled princess who gambled and lost." Tuck couldn't help a grim smirk at the memory. Clearly, his former sister-in-law had expected a hefty financial settlement.

"She's holding a grudge," said Jackson. "Do you think she'd harm him?"

"She probably wants to. But that would require risk and effort. She's lazy."

"Yeah," Jackson agreed. "I'm starting to wonder if he was kidnapped."

Tuck frowned. He'd been picturing Dixon on a tropical beach somewhere. If his brother was in trouble, then Tuck's anger at him was completely misplaced.

"Maybe he was forced to write that letter to your dad," said Jackson.

"Tell me you're not serious."

"Who saw him last?"

Tuck nodded to his closed office door, his thoughts moving to Amber. She'd kept him carefully at arm's length since the night in New York, but he was practically obsessing over her.

"His assistant, Amber," he told Jackson. "He was in the office for a few hours the day he left."

"Can you call her in?"

"Sure." Tuck came to his feet. "But I've already pumped her for information. She's the one who gave me his password. He didn't tell her where he was going."

He crossed to the door and drew it open, walking into the outer office.

Amber was at her desk, profile to him as she typed on the keyboard.

"Can you join us?" he asked.

She stopped typing and glanced up, her blue gaze meeting his. There was a wariness there, which he chalked up to the kisses in New York. Could she tell he wanted to do it again?

He was dying to do it again. He feared it was written all over his expression every time he looked her way.

"Sure." She smoothed out her expression and pushed back her chair.

As usual, her outfit was straitlaced, a navy blazer over a matching pleated skirt and a white blouse. Her spike pumps were bright blue with a slash of white across the toe. They appeared simple by Amber-footwear standards, but they still struck him as sleekly sexy. Or maybe it was only his fevered imagination.

As she rose, he caught a glimpse of lace beneath the neckline of her blouse and his desire went into hyperdrive. He warned himself to bide his time until Dixon returned. When things were back to normal, he'd try approaching her again. Amber would no longer be working for him then.

"What do you need?" she asked as she passed by him.

"Jackson has a couple of questions." Tuck fell into step behind her.

"What kind of questions?"

"About Dixon."

She twisted her head, pausing just outside the office door. "What about Dixon?"

Did he detect guilt in her eyes? Was she nervous?

"The usual questions." He found himself scrutinizing her expression.

"What are the usual questions?"

"Shall we find out?"

"I've told you everything I know."

"You say that in a way that makes me wonder."

"Words strung into a sentence make you suspicious?"

"You're jumpy," he said.

"I'm annoyed."

"You have no reason to be annoyed."

"I've got work to do."

"So do I. And none of our work gets easier until Dixon is back."

Her eyes narrowed. “He shouldn’t be your crutch.”

“He’s everybody’s crutch. Do you know where he is?”

“No.”

He gestured her forward. “Then, let’s go talk to Jackson.”

Amber squared her shoulders and moved into the office.

Jackson rose. “Nice to see you again, Amber.”

“Why do I feel like this is an interrogation?” she asked.

“I have that effect on people,” said Jackson.

“You should stop.” She took one of the armchairs in the grouping.

“I’ll keep that in mind.”

For some reason, the exchange grated on Tuck. Jackson wasn’t flirting with her. But he was joking with her and Tuck didn’t like it.

“Your questions?” he asked Jackson.

Jackson caught his gaze and looked puzzled.

“Sure,” said Jackson, obviously waiting for Tuck to sit down.

Tuck perched on the arm of a chair. He folded his arms over his chest.

It took Jackson a moment to move his attention back to Amber.

“I’m sure you’ll agree,” he said to her, “that Dixon has been gone longer than any of us expected.”

“How long did we expect him to be gone?” she asked.

“Did he tell you how long he’d be gone?”

Amber glanced fleetingly at Tuck. “His letter said a month.”

“It’s been a month.”

“Almost.”

“No phone call? No postcard?”

“Who sends a postcard these days?”

“People who want you to know they’re having a good time and wish you were there.”

Amber’s gaze hardened. “I doubt he’s having a good time.”

Tuck could almost hear Jackson’s senses go on alert.

“Why?” Jackson asked.

"You know about his ex-wife." Amber wasn't asking a question.

"I do."

"Then you know he's recovering from her treachery."

"Treachery?"

"What would you call it?"

"Infidelity."

"Okay."

Jackson paused. "What was your relationship with Dixon?"

"Hey," Tuck protested. "Amber's not on trial."

Jackson shot him a look of astonishment. "Should I be doing this without you?"

"He was my boss," said Amber. "Full stop. And if one more person insinuates it was something inappropriate, I'm walking out the door."

"Who else insinuated that?"

"Back off," said Tuck. This was getting them nowhere. It was only annoying Amber, and rightly so. He didn't blame her for being ticked off.

"Who else?" asked Jackson.

"Tuck." She slid him an angry glance.

He held up his hands in surrender. He hadn't considered anything of the sort for quite some time now.

"And Jamison," said Amber.

Jackson's tone slipped up in obvious surprise. "Jamison thought you were having an affair with his son?"

"Only because Jamison was having an—" Amber snapped her mouth shut.

Jackson blinked.

Tuck rose to his feet.

Amber stiffened her spine.

"You're going to have to finish that sentence," said Tuck.

She shook her head.

"I insist."

"We all know what she was going to say," Jackson said.

"I didn't say it," said Amber.

"My father was having an affair?"

She glared at Tuck. "Let it go."

"With who?" he demanded. Tuck's first reaction was that it couldn't be true. Then again, it absolutely could be true. Lots of high-powered, self-gratifying people cheated. Why not his father?

"It's not for me to say," Amber responded. "I found out by accident. In fact, I don't even know for sure."

"Who do you suspect?"

Who it was might have no bearing on Dixon's situation. Then again, it might. Had Dixon known about the affair?

"That would be gossip," said Amber.

"My father is in the hospital. My brother is *missing*. Gossip already."

She glanced from Tuck to Jackson and back again. "Can I swear you two to secrecy?"

"Amber," Tuck all but shouted.

This wasn't a negotiation. There were no conditions. She was answering the question.

"Yes," said Jackson. He glared at Tuck. "We'll keep it to ourselves. As you say, it's speculation. It would be wrong for us to act on hearsay."

"Margaret," said Amber.

"His Margaret?" Tuck asked.

"Who is Margaret?" asked Jackson.

"His assistant," said Amber.

"But—" Tuck couldn't wrap his head around it. Margaret Smithers could best be described as matronly. She was middle-aged, slightly overweight, her hair was partly gray and her clothes were polyester.

"Expecting a blond supermodel?" asked Amber.

Tuck wasn't about to admit that was true. "I was expecting him to be faithful to my mother."

"Did Dixon know?" asked Jackson, his thoughts obviously moving along the same lines as Tuck's.

Dixon had just been a victim of infidelity. Finding out about their father might have angered him enough to leave. Tuck couldn't help but wonder if he planned to stay gone.

"No," said Amber.

"How can you be sure?" asked Tuck. It would at least have been some kind of explanation.

Amber had to think about it for a moment. "I'm as sure as I can be. I didn't figure it out until the heart attack. And Dixon never acted as if he knew."

"How did you figure it out?" asked Jackson.

"The way Margaret acted when Jamison collapsed," said Amber. "She mentioned they'd had wine together the night before. Then when she realized what she'd said, she panicked."

"You were with Jamison when it happened?" asked Jackson.

"I was in his office. He was upset, grilling me about Dixon. When I wouldn't tell him anything, he got really angry." She fell to silence, and her shoulders drooped. A cloud came over her eyes. "Maybe I should have told…"

Tuck looked to Jackson. Both men waited, but she didn't elaborate.

"Should have told what?" Jackson prompted in a soft voice.

Amber refocused on him. "Nothing."

"What was he asking?"

"Where Dixon went."

"But you didn't tell him."

"No."

"Tell us."

She drew back. "I don't know."

"You just admitted that you did," said Tuck.

She shook her head in vigorous denial.

"You said maybe you should have told him, but you didn't tell him."

"That's not what I—"

"No," said Tuck. He kept his tone carefully even, but inwardly he was furious. She'd been lying to him. She'd watched him struggle all these weeks. She'd pretended to help him, when all the while the solution had been at her fingertips.

"You can't walk it back," he said. "You know where Dixon went. Tell me. Tell me right this second."

She compressed her lips, staring at him, her expression a combination of guilt and defiance.

"That's an order," he said. "Tell me, or you're fired—"

"Tuck," Jackson cut in.

"No," said Tuck. "She's sat back and let Tucker Transportation fall down around my ears. She doesn't get to do that and keep her job."

"I can't," she protested.

"Then, you're fired."

Five

Tuck's final words echoed inside Amber's ears.

She put her compact car into Park outside her town house, set the brake and gripped the steering wheel. She was home an hour early, and it felt surreal. The sun was too high in the sky and kids were still playing in the park across the street, whooping it up on the slide and the jungle gym.

Fired. She'd been fired from Tucker Transportation. She had no job. She had no paycheck. Her savings might take her through the next month, but she had mortgage payments, utility payments, phone bills and food bills.

She cursed the new shoes on her feet. She'd worn them for the first time today and she couldn't take them back. Then again, they were gorgeous and they'd been on sale. And, really, how much would a refund help? It would barely fill up her gas tank.

She couldn't waste time worrying about might-have-beens. She had to get it together. She had to start job hunting right away.

The front door opened and Jade stood there, looking out, her rounded belly pressing against an oversize plaid shirt. Amber was reminded that she also had Jade and the baby to worry about. Not that it changed her plans.

She'd update her résumé tonight and get out job hunting first thing tomorrow. It would have been nice to have Dixon as a reference. She sure couldn't use Tuck.

She turned off the engine, trying unsuccessfully to banish his image from her mind. He'd been angry. That much was certainly clear. But he'd looked hurt, too, seeming disappointed that her loyalty was to Dixon. She wished she could have given Tuck what he wanted, but she couldn't serve them both.

She stepped out of the car and waved to Jade as she walked up the stepping-stones. The sage and asters were barely hanging on. The other blooms had faded away, and only the leaves remained. October was not exactly a cheerful month.

As she approached the door, she pasted a smile on her face. "How are you feeling?"

"Huge."

Amber widened her smile at the joke.

"I made an appointment at the community clinic," said Jade, as she stepped back from the doorway.

"That's good." Amber had been insistent that Jade get proper medical care. "When is the appointment?"

"I told them my due date and they got me in tomorrow."

Amber glanced at Jade's stomach. "I guess they know there's no time to waste."

"Being pregnant is not an illness."

"But you want a healthy baby."

"Oof." Jade's hand went to her stomach. "This one's healthy, all right. It's got a kick like a soccer player."

"I can drive you to the appointment," said Amber. She'd be happier if she heard firsthand what the doctor had to say.

"I can take the bus."

Amber dumped her purse and headed for the living room. "It's no trouble. I can afford to take a little time off."

"Are you sure?"

"Positive."

Amber would be taking more than just a little time off. But she didn't see any need to say so immediately. Hopefully, she'd have a new job lined up before she had to share the news about losing this one.

"Are you hungry?" she asked Jade.

"I made macaroni casserole."

Amber couldn't hide her surprise. "You cooked?"

Not that macaroni casserole was exactly gourmet, but Jade

had never been handy in the kitchen, nor particularly self-motivated when it came to household chores.

Jade grinned proudly as they walked to the kitchen. "It's all ready to pop into the oven."

"That sounds delicious. Thanks."

Jade turned on the oven while Amber set out plates and cutlery and let her optimism build. She had five solid years of work at Tucker Transportation. She'd built up her administrative skill set, and surely that would be transferable to any number of companies. Maybe she could gloss over her reasons for leaving. She might even be able to use Margaret as a reference.

She hoped Tuck wouldn't be vindictive and spread word around the company that she was fired. But she really had no idea how he'd handle it. He was pretty angry right now.

There was a sudden knock on the front door.

"Expecting someone?" asked Jade.

"Not me. You?"

"Nobody knows I'm here."

Amber went for the door, suspecting it was a neighbor, maybe Sally Duncan from next door. She was on the townhouse council and loved to complain. Perhaps old Mr. Purvis was barbecuing on his patio again.

Amber had voted to repeal the prohibition on barbecues at the last council meeting. Sure, the smoke was annoying. But who in their right mind would ban hot dogs and hamburgers?

She swung open the door, startled to find Tuck standing on her porch. He was frowning, eyes narrowed. Worry immediately clenched her stomach.

"What do you want?" she asked him.

"To talk."

"I have nothing else to say."

"After you left, Jackson pointed out the error of my ways."

She didn't want to hope. But she couldn't help herself. Was Tuck offering her job back?

"I came here to give you another chance," he said.

She waited.

"You being gone helps neither of us," he said.

She had to agree with that. But she doubted he cared about helping her.

"Another chance to what?" she prompted.

"What can you tell me about Dixon?"

"I've told you everything—"

"Well, hello there." Jade arrived, breaking in with a breezy tone. "Are you one of Amber's neighbors?"

Tuck's brow shot up as he took in the pregnant Jade.

"He's my boss," said Amber, instantly realizing it was no longer true. But before she could correct the statement, Jade was talking again.

"Really? Very nice to meet you. I'm Amber's sister, Jade." Jade stuck out her hand.

"Jade, this really isn't a good time."

"Tuck Tucker," said Tuck as he shook Jade's hand.

"Are you hungry?" asked Jade.

"No, he's not," Amber quickly responded.

"I need to borrow your sister for a few minutes," Tuck said to Jade.

"Does she need to go back to work?" asked Jade.

"No," Tuck and Amber answered simultaneously.

"I just need to speak with her," said Tuck.

"Oh," said Jade, glancing between them, obviously picking up on their discomfort. "Then, I'll leave you two alone."

As Jade withdrew, Amber moved onto the porch, pulling the door closed behind her. It was cold outside, but she wanted to get this over with.

"The job market's very tight out there," said Tuck.

"Are you trying to frighten me?"

"I'm asking you to be realistic. I need to talk to my brother."

"I promised him I wouldn't tell a soul. That included his family."

"So you admit you know where he is."

"I don't know with any certainty where he is."

"Why are you talking in riddles?"

She reached behind herself for the doorknob. “I’ve told you what I can.”

“I can’t imagine Dixon wants you to be fired.”

“I can’t imagine he does, either.”

Dixon had always given her top-notch performance evaluations. He’d praised her work, often saying he didn’t know how he’d live without her. She liked to think he wouldn’t want her fired.

“Don’t make me do it,” said Tuck.

“I’m not *making* you do anything.”

“Ignoring an order is gross insubordination.”

“Betraying a confidence is worse.”

He leaned in. “Circumstances have changed since you made that promise.”

She knew they had. But she also knew Dixon’s doctor had told him to get away from the pressures of Tucker Transportation.

“Amber.” Tuck reached out, his hand encircling her upper arm. “I *need* this, please.”

His touch brought a rush of memories—the strength of his embrace, the taste of his lips and the scent of his skin. Suddenly, she was off balance, and she felt herself sway toward him. Her hand moved to steady herself, her palm coming up against his chest.

He groaned deep in his throat. “I don’t want to fight with you.”

She jerked her hand away, but he was faster, engulfing it in his own, pressing it firmly back against his chest.

His tone was gravelly. “Don’t make me fight with you.”

She battled the desire rising in her body. She wanted nothing more and nothing less than to collapse into Tuck’s arms and kiss him until every other thought was driven from her brain.

She met his gaze. “I’ve told you everything I can.”

His expression turned mocking. “And you *still* claim there’s nothing going on between you and Dixon.”

“I’ll claim it as many times as it takes. It’s the truth.”

“Yet you’ll give up your job for him?”

"I'll give up my job for a principle."

He tugged her closer, voice going quiet. "You sure about that?"

She enunciated each syllable. "Positive."

He kissed her.

She was so surprised that she didn't fight it. Her lips were pliable under his—soft, welcoming—and, for a second, she kissed him back. Her brain screeched at her to stop. But his embrace was oddly comforting. His kiss was tender. And the warmth of his chest seemed to make its way into her heart.

Then reason asserted itself. She forced herself to push against him, staggering back and thudding against the closed door. They stared at each other. Her chest rose and fell with labored breaths.

"I had to be sure," he said.

"Sure of *what*?"

"That you're not in love with my brother."

"Go away." She scrunched her eyes shut to block him out. "Just go away, and stay gone. I think I might hate you."

He didn't make a sound.

After a moment, she opened one eye. His back was to her and he was halfway down the path, striding toward a sleek black sports car.

Thank goodness he was leaving. Thank goodness he was out of her life. She could get a new job. She *would* get a new job. The last place on earth she wanted to be was working for Tuck.

The door opened behind her.

"Amber?" Jade's voice was hesitant.

"Yes." Amber shook some sense into herself.

"Your boss is your boyfriend?"

Amber turned. "What? No."

"You just kissed him."

"That?" Amber waved it away. "That was nothing. He was being a jerk, is all. He fired me."

"He *what*?"

"We had a disagreement. No. More a difference of opinion. I'd call it a difference of principles and values. He's not a man I want to work for." Amber paused. "I'm fine with the way things turned out."

She was fine. At least she would be fine.

"What will you do?" There was worry in Jade's expression.

Amber linked her arm with her sister's and moved them both inside. "I'll get another job. This was a good job, but it's not the only job. I have skills and experience. Maybe I'll even make more money."

"You sound confident."

"I *am* confident."

Maybe her leaving Tucker Transportation was inevitable. Jamison had most certainly planned to fire her before his heart attack. If she looked at it like that, she'd actually been granted an extra month with Tuck at the helm. But it was doomed to end one way or the other.

Dixon would eventually come back and he'd probably take her side. But Jamison was the president of the company. Eventually, he'd recover fully and overrule Dixon. And with Tuck now on Jamison's side… Well, this was definitely the time for her to move on.

Tuck's workload had gotten completely out of control. Without Amber as the gatekeeper, he was inundated with problems, big and small. He had a temporary assistant, Sandy Heath, borrowed from the finance department, but she mostly just asked him a lot of questions, slowing him down instead of speeding him up.

Jackson had followed a new dead-end lead to Cancún, and another manager had resigned this morning. They were bleeding employees. His father's recovery was going more slowly than expected. Jamison might not return to work at all.

"Sandy?" Tuck called through the open door.

"Yes?"

He could hear her stand and move to the door.

"Is Lucas Steele on his way up?"

Sandy paused in the doorway. "I don't know."

Tuck took a beat. "Could you find out?"

"Sure."

Tuck glanced at his watch to confirm the time. "Did you tell him ten?"

"I believe so. I mean, I called when you asked me to. But I got his voice mail."

"Did you try his assistant?"

Sandy paused. "I'll do that now."

"Great." Just great. Tuck couldn't even get his operations director into his office when they only worked three floors apart.

He came to his feet. "Never mind."

She looked puzzled. "You don't want Lucas?"

"I'll go down."

"I can—"

"I'll find him."

"I'm sorry."

Tuck relaxed his expression. "Don't worry about it."

There was no point in being annoyed with Sandy because she wasn't Amber. Only Amber was Amber, and she was ridiculously good at her job.

He went to the elevator and rode down to twenty-nine. The hallway on that floor was linoleum rather than carpet. The offices were smaller than on the executive floor, and there was far more activity. It was the nerve center of the company, where every company conveyance was tracked on a series of wall-mounted screens, with information on every single shipment available with a few keystrokes. Tuck had come to like it here.

Lucas's office was at the far end of the hallway. It was large but utilitarian, its numerous tables cluttered with maps and reports, keyboards and screens. Tuck knew Lucas had a desk in there somewhere, but he wasn't sure the man ever sat down.

"Hey, boss," Lucas greeted from behind a table.

One of his female staff members was working beside him, clicking keys and watching a set of three monitors.

"The *Red Earth* is back on schedule," the woman said without looking up. "They'll make their 6:00 a.m. port time."

"Good," said Lucas. "Need me?" he asked Tuck.

"You didn't get Sandy's voice mail?"

Lucas glanced guiltily at his desk phone. "We've been slammed this morning."

"Not a problem," said Tuck. "Got a minute?"

"Absolutely. Gwen, can you make sure we get the fuel agreement signatures sent? We have until close of business in Berlin."

"Will do," said Gwen, again without looking up.

Lucas led the way out of his office, turning immediately into a small meeting room along the hall.

"What's up?" he asked Tuck, closing the door behind them.

"I feel as if we should sit down for this," said Tuck.

"Bad news?" Lucas crossed his arms over his chest. "Are you firing me?"

Tuck scoffed out a laugh at the absurdity of the statement. "I'm promoting you."

"Yeah, right." Lucas waited, alert.

"I'm serious," said Tuck.

"Serious about what?"

"I'm promoting you."

It took Lucas a beat to answer. "Why? To what? There's nothing above director."

"Nothing in operations," said Tuck.

"Right," said Lucas, as if he'd just proved his point.

"Vice president," said Tuck.

"Are you running a fever?"

"I need you upstairs."

"I'm no vice president." Lucas gave an exaggerated shudder. "You think I am?"

"Yes."

Tuck pressed his lips together. "Only because they gave me the title."

"You're nuts."

"I'm serious."

"Okay." Lucas braced his feet slightly apart. "Vice president of *what*?"

"I don't know."

"I can see you've really thought this through."

"Executive vice president."

"That's *your* title."

"I'm acting president."

Lucas's arms moved to his sides. "I suppose you are."

"I'm drownin' up there. Dixon's completely dropped off the planet, and Dad's recovery is pushed back. I know it's not your first choice, but what am I supposed to do?"

"Hire someone."

"I'm hiring you."

"Hire someone else."

"I will. For your job."

"You don't need to hire anyone for my job. Gwen can do it. She can probably do it better than me."

Tuck didn't feel any need to respond to the statement. Lucas had just made the next argument for him.

"Yeah, yeah," said Lucas. "I know what you're thinking."

"What am I thinking?" Tuck asked.

"That you can pick me up and plunk me into some fancy office, and the operations department won't even notice I'm gone."

Tuck fought a smirk. "Your words, not mine."

"They're true."

"That's good."

"I wouldn't have the first idea of what to do upstairs," said Lucas.

"And you think *I* do?"

"You're a Tucker."

"You're the last one left," said Tuck.

"The last one of what?"

"The last director. The others quit."

"Not Oscar?"

"Yesterday. The rumor mill now has Dixon pegged as an

embezzler who will bring down the company, and the head-hunters are out in force."

Lucas frowned. "There's no chance he actually…?"

Tuck was astonished. *"You, too?"*

"No. Not really. What would be his motivation? Plus, you'd have noticed the missing millions by now and reported it. Law enforcement would be crawling all over this place."

Tuck couldn't help but admire Lucas's combination of faith and hard, cold analysis. "He has no motivation. And he didn't do anything illegal."

"I gotta agree," said Lucas.

"Doesn't mean I won't knock his block off."

Lucas pulled out a molded plastic chair and sat down at the rectangular meeting table.

Tuck took the seat across from him.

"You're serious," said Lucas.

"Completely. While Amber was here, it was doable, marginal but doable. Without her, I can't keep it going. We've lost three major accounts since Zachary left."

"You think he's poaching them."

"I know he's poaching them. What I don't know is how to make it stop. I mean, maybe I can make it stop, if I can find the time to make some calls and build up some relationships. But I don't even have time to breathe. I need Dixon, and I need him now."

"I thought Jackson was looking."

"He hit a dead end. It's dead end number eight, I think."

"Hire another investigative firm."

"There's nobody better than Jackson. If only—"

Tuck's thoughts went back to Amber. Usually, when he thought about her, it was about their kisses, particularly that last kiss. A woman didn't kiss like that, especially not in the middle of a fight, if she didn't have a thing for the man. Amber had to be attracted to him on some level, and the knowledge made his skin itch.

"If only what?" asked Lucas.

"She knows something. She can get Dixon back for me."

"Who?"

"Amber."

Lucas pulled back in his chair, a speculative expression coming over his face.

"Not like that," said Tuck. "Not at *all* like that. She was his confidential assistant and he confided in her."

"What did he tell her?"

"She's not talking. I ordered her. Then I fired her. But she's not talking."

"Bribe?" asked Lucas.

"She just gave up her job over integrity."

"Blackmail, then?"

"With what? She's as straight up as they come. The only thing outrageous about her is her shoes."

"Her shoes?"

"You've never noticed?"

Lucas shook his head. "Can't say that I have."

"I don't see how I blackmail her over red glitter stilettoes." Though Tuck would love to have pictures of them.

"Can't believe I missed that."

Tuck forced his mind back to the job. "Will you do it?"

Lucas curled his fingertips against the table. "Temporarily."

Tuck felt a rush of relief. "I hope that's all I'll need. Even together, we can't replace Dixon."

"No, we can't."

"I'm going to find him."

"You should definitely bribe her."

"She'll never go for it."

"You don't know that until you ask."

"Yes, I do."

If Amber was willing to trade ethics for money, she'd never have let him fire her.

Amber sat down at her kitchen table, taking up where she'd left off scrolling through an employment website. Jade was across from her, writing her way through a practice math exam. The coffeepot was between them and their breakfast dishes were piled in the sink.

Jade had offered to clean up later while Amber made the rounds of some more major companies in the city. Surprisingly, after three weeks in Chicago, Jade was still following her new life plan. She was rising every morning with her alarm, eating healthy and studying for the GED test she hoped to pass before the baby was born.

By contrast, Amber's new life plan was completely falling apart. She'd applied for dozens of jobs, had landed only three interviews and had so far been beaten by other candidates on two of them. Every morning, she told herself not to lose hope. But she'd already dipped into her savings to make the month's mortgage payment. Other bills were coming due, including Jade's appointments at the community clinic.

"You look nice today," said Jade. "Very professional." She nodded approvingly at Amber's blazer and skirt.

"Focus on the test," said Amber.

"I bet you get an offer."

"That would be nice." Amber wasn't going to let Jade see her worry.

"Ooh." Jade's hand went to her stomach. "That was a good one."

"I bet it's a boy," said Amber. She copied and pasted a promising-looking job ad into her open spreadsheet.

"Girl," said Jade. "But a soccer player."

"Boy," said Amber. "A placekicker for the Bears. Big money in that."

"You think we'll need Junior's money?"

Amber was beginning to think they'd need it before Junior even started preschool.

"I doubt we will," said Jade. "We're both going to get jobs—good jobs, high-powered jobs. We'll get promoted up the ladder and make fortunes."

Amber couldn't help but smile. She liked it when Jade was optimistic. "Dreamer."

"I am," said Jade. "For the first time in my— Ouch. I think that one went through the uprights."

The phone rang. Amber couldn't control the lurch of anticipation that hit her stomach. It could be another interview, or possibly a job offer from Pine Square Furniture. Please, let it be a job offer. Pine Square Furniture paid quite a bit less than what she'd made at Tucker Transportation, but she'd jump at anything right now.

As Amber started to rise, Jade leaned back and lifted the receiver.

"Hello?"

Amber held her breath.

"Oh, hi, Dr. Norris."

Amber's disappointment was acute. She turned to hide her expression from Jade, rising and pretending to check the printer for paper.

"Okay," Jade said into the phone.

Amber reminded herself these things took time. She could make it a few more weeks, even a couple of months. She hadn't really expected to find a job the next day, had she?

"Which test?" There was worry in Jade's tone.

Amber turned back.

"Is that a problem?" Jade's worried gaze met Amber's.

Amber quickly returned to the table, sitting down in the chair beside Jade.

"That sounds scary," said Jade.

"What is it?" Amber whispered.

Jade's eyes went glassy with the beginnings of tears.

"What?" Amber said louder. "What's wrong?"

Jade unexpectedly pushed the receiver at her, nearly dropping it between them.

Amber scrambled to get it to her ear. "Dr. Norris? This is Amber."

"Hello, Amber. Is Jade all right?"

"She's upset. She's okay. What did you tell her?"

"I have a concern with her blood pressure."

Amber had known that. "Yes."

They'd talked about Jade taking some medication to keep it down in the last few weeks of her pregnancy.

"I'm afraid the follow-up tests aren't encouraging."

Amber rubbed Jade's shoulder. "Is everything okay with the baby?"

"So far, yes. Jade has a condition called preeclampsia. It's serious. I'm recommending you bring her into the hospital."

The hospital? "How serious?"

Jade sniffed and reached for a tissue.

"I'd like to monitor Jade's health and the baby's health."

"Overnight? Until the medication kicks in?"

"Until the birth, I'm afraid. We can't take this condition lightly. There are risks to the placenta, organ damage for Jade, even stroke."

Amber squeezed Jade's hand. "How soon should I bring her in?"

"Is she still having headaches?"

Amber moved the phone from her mouth. "Headache?" she asked Jade.

"It's not bad," said Jade.

"Yes," Amber said to the doctor.

"Then, let's not wait. This morning if you can."

"We can," said Amber.

"My office will make the arrangements."

"Thank you." Amber ended the call.

"So I have to go back?" asked Jade.

"Yes. The doctor says they need to monitor you. She wants you in the hospital."

"The *hospital*?"

"She's worried about your blood pressure."

"But they said there was medicine."

"We can ask more questions when we get there." Amber couldn't help feeling a sense of urgency.

"How long will I have to stay?"

"It might be for a while. We don't want to take any chances. This is what's best for you, and what's best for the baby." Amber stood. "Let's go pack a few things."

Jade gestured to her books. "But I'm studying."

"I'll bet you can study in the hospital. In fact, it might be the perfect place to study. There'll be nothing else for you to do. They'll cook for you. They'll clean for you."

"Hospital food?"

"I'll smuggle you in a pizza."

Assuming Jade was allowed to eat pizza. Amber drew Jade to her feet.

"I can't do this," said Jade. "I can't just up and leave for the hospital at a moment's notice."

"Sometimes it works that way."

Jade glanced around the kitchen. "How can I, what can I—Oh, no." She grasped tightly onto Amber's arms.

Amber's heart leaped. "Is something wrong?"

"The money."

"What money?"

"The *money*, Amber. This is going to cost a fortune. Where will I get the money?"

"Don't worry about that."

"I have to worry about it."

"Worrying won't help anything. Not you, and definitely not the baby." Amber would have to do the worrying for them.

"But—"

"We'll borrow it. Then we'll pay it back." Amber struggled to put confidence in her voice.

"I'm so sorry."

"This isn't your fault. You're doing so well." Amber motioned to the books. "You've been studying. You've been eating right. You're here. You need to keep doing everything you can to give your baby the best possible chance."

"I'm scared." But Jade started to move.

"I know. I'm not saying it isn't unsettling. But it's going to be fine. Everything is going to be fine."

Amber would get Jade to the hospital, and then she'd talk to her bank. She had some equity in her town house and a decent credit rating. Once she found a job, she would qualify for a loan. So she'd find a job. She'd find one fast. She'd flip burgers if that was what it took.

Six

Tuck knew a losing hand when he was dealt one. But he also knew he couldn't walk away from this. For better or worse, and so far it was definitely worse, the company was his responsibility.

It was Saturday afternoon and he'd parked down the block from Amber's town house, waiting for her car to appear. The block was neat and bright, lawns trimmed, gardens tended, with kids playing in the park and people walking their dogs. The homes were compact, four to a building, with very little traffic passing on the street out front.

He figured he'd have the best chance if he tried to reason with her in person. It was too easy for her to hang up a phone. And he doubted she'd answer a text or email. Plus, her expression might help him, give him a signal as to which tactic might sway her and which was a nonstarter.

He knew it wasn't about self-interest for her. And he couldn't imagine she'd have one iota of sympathy for him. But maybe she'd care about the other employees. Maybe she would care that the demise of Tucker Transportation would be job losses and financial ruin for the families of her former coworkers. The way he saw it, that was his best hope.

He spotted her silver hatchback pull up in front of the town house, and he quickly exited his sports car. While she hopped from the driver's seat he approached from the side.

Dressed in a pair of navy slacks and a striped pullover with a matching blazer, she was lithe and graceful as she moved across the sidewalk. Her hair was in a neat braid, while her low-heeled boots were a sexy purple suede. She was compellingly beautiful in the cool sunshine, her profile perky, her skin smooth as silk.

She hadn't seen him yet, so she had a smile on her face. He supposed he'd change that soon enough.

It didn't take long. She caught a glimpse of him, squinted at him and then frowned.

"Hello, Amber," he said, covering the last few paces between them.

Her glance flicked behind him as if seeking context. "What are you doing here, Tuck?"

"Been out shopping?" he asked conversationally. It seemed like a reasonable guess for a Saturday afternoon.

"I've been visiting—" She stopped herself. "What do you want?"

"I need to talk to you."

"I don't have time to talk." She started for the walkway that led to her front door.

"It won't take long."

She turned. "Then, let me be more blunt. I have all the time in the world, but I don't care to spend any of it with you."

"You're still angry."

"What was your first clue?"

"I didn't want things to go this way."

"Goodbye, Tuck." She took a backward step.

"Dixon is still missing."

She shrugged.

"It's been over six weeks. I'm getting worried."

"He can take care of himself."

Under normal circumstances, Dixon could take excellent care of himself. But these weren't normal circumstances.

"Who takes a six-week vacation?"

"Lots of people."

"Not my brother."

Even if their father had been healthy and at the helm, Dixon would never have left for this long, especially not without contacting them. Tuck's focus had been on Tucker Transportation, but he was becoming genuinely worried about his brother.

"Maybe you don't know him as well as you think you do," said Amber.

"Clearly, I don't. Why don't you enlighten me?"

"Why should I know him any better than you?"

"You know him."

It was in her eyes.

"You knew why he left," said Tuck. "And you know where he went." Tuck believed there was no romance between her and Dixon. But there was something—a closeness, respect, confidence.

"He doesn't want to talk to you?"

"He's got nothing against me."

Tuck and Dixon might not be the closest brothers in the world. But they weren't estranged. They weren't fighting. There was no particular animosity between them.

Tuck stepped forward. "Things have gotten worse since you…left."

"You mean since I was fired."

"Yeah, that." He didn't know why he'd tried to soften the words. They both knew what had happened. "We're losing accounts. We're losing staff. We've gone from high profitability to a projected loss for next month."

There was no sympathy in her blue eyes. "You might want to do something about that."

"I'm worried about the employees," he said, ignoring her jab. "If this goes on much longer, people could lose their jobs."

"What does that have to do with me? Considering I already lost mine."

"I'm appealing to your basic sense of humanity."

"While I'm still standing on my basic sense of ethics and values."

He eased closer. "Where is he, Amber?"

"I don't know."

"What do you know?"

She raised her chin. "That he didn't want me to tell you anything."

"That was weeks ago."

"I haven't heard anything to contradict it."

"So you haven't heard from him?"

She drew back in obvious surprise. "No."

"Does he know how to contact you?"

"He'd probably try to call me at my desk."

"Touché."

"He knows how to contact you, too, Tuck. If he wanted to talk to you, he'd call." She turned to go.

"What about an emergency?" Tuck called out. He could taste failure, bitter in the back of his mouth. "Can you get a message to him? That's all I'm asking. Get a message to him. You can name your price."

She stopped. Then she pivoted, gaping at him in clear astonishment. "My *price*?"

"Anything you want." He could feel his last chance slipping away. "What do you want?"

To Tuck's immense relief, she actually looked intrigued.

"You'd pay me to get a message to Dixon."

"Yes."

She seemed to think about it. "What would you want me to say?"

"You'll do it?"

Had Lucas actually been right? Was money going to sway her?

"What would you want me to say?" she asked again.

"Tell him about my father's heart attack and tell him I'm destroying the company."

She looked a little surprised by the last statement. "You want to make certain he comes home."

"I want to make certain he knows the cost of staying away."

"I'm not going to lie for you."

"It's not a lie."

"It is. You're not destroying the company. You've hit a rough patch, sure, but—"

"You haven't been there."

It was every bit as bad as he was making it sound.

"You're exaggerating," she said.

They could have this debate all day long and get nowhere. He had a toehold on a yes here, and he didn't want to give her a chance to back out.

"What'll it cost me?" he asked.

"You're talking about a flat-out cash bribe?"

"If that's what works."

She looked skeptical. "And I'd only have to tell him about your father."

"And that I'm destroying the company."

"I'm not using the word *destroy*."

"Then, tell him I've projected a loss for next month." Tuck knew that would come as a colossal shock to Dixon. He'd be on the first plane home.

He could see the debate going on behind her eyes.

"How much?" he asked.

What would she ask for? Five figures, six? He'd pay whatever she wanted.

"My job back," she said.

He hadn't been prepared for that. And he was shocked she'd be willing. "You want to work for me again?"

"I want to work for Dixon again."

"Job's yours," he said. He'd be thrilled to have her back. In fact, he felt guilty that her request was so modest. He moved a little closer. "You have to know you've got me over a barrel?"

"Do you want me to ask for something more?"

He did. If nothing else, he was curious. "Yeah. Go wild."

She hesitated.

He raised a brow, waiting.

"All right." She withdrew a paper from her purse, unfolding it. "Since you insist."

"What's that?" He tried to look, but she pulled it toward her chest.

"You can give me a signing bonus."

"How much?"

"Twenty-eight thousand, two hundred and sixty-three dollars."

Now she really had him curious.

"Where did that number come from?"

"None of your business." She refolded the paper and stuffed it back in her purse.

"Seriously. What are you paying for?"

"Seriously. None of your business."

Tuck told himself to shut up and take the victory. "You'll call him."

"I will."

"I mean now."

"Right now?"

He gave a sharp nod.

"I suppose." She turned again for the front door.

He followed and she twisted her head to look at him.

"You don't trust me?"

"I do. I don't." No, that wasn't true. He couldn't imagine she'd lie about making the call. "I do trust you. But I want to see what happens."

She unlocked the front door, pushing it open. "I don't know for sure where he is. I didn't lie to you about that. But he did leave an emergency number."

Tuck wanted to ask exactly how bad things had to get before she decided it was an emergency. But he didn't want to start another argument.

He stayed silent, and she dropped her purse on a table in the small foyer and extracted her phone, dialing as she moved into the living room.

"Did he get a special cell phone?" Tuck asked. That made the most sense.

Amber shook her head, listening as the call obviously rang through.

She sat down on a cream-colored loveseat and crossed her legs. Tuck perched on an end of the sofa at a right angle to her. It faced a gas fireplace and a row of small watercolor seascapes.

"Hello," said Amber. "Can you connect me to Dixon Tucker's room?"

A hotel, obviously. Tuck wanted to know where. He wished he could see the area code.

"He's not?" asked Amber, her tone sharper.

Tuck focused on her expression.

She was frowning. "I don't understand. When did he do that?"

Tuck didn't want to be suspicious, but he couldn't help but wonder if she was playing him. Was she going to pretend she'd tried to get Dixon but failed?

"That's less than a week. Did he say where he was going?" She met Tuck's eyes, sitting up straight and bracing her feet on the carpet. Either something was actually wrong, or Amber had a great future in acting. "Yes. I understand."

"What?" he asked her.

"Thank you," she said into the phone. "Goodbye."

"What did they say? Who was that? Where's Dixon?"

Amber set the phone onto the sofa cushion beside her. "He left."

"Left *where*?"

"Scottsdale."

"Arizona?"

"It's called Highland Luminance."

It struck Tuck as an odd name. "A hotel?"

"A wellness retreat."

The words weren't making sense.

"What's that?" Tuck asked. "And what was he doing there?"

"Getting well. At least he was supposed to be getting well.

But he left." Concern furrowed her brow. "He left after only a few days. Why would he do that?"

"Why would he go there in the first place?"

Sure, Dixon's divorce had been ugly. But people went through ugly divorces all the time.

"For help," said Amber. "They have a spa, yoga, fresh air and peace, organic food, emotional and physical therapy."

"You're trying to tell me that my brother took off to Arizona for organic food and yoga."

"I'm not *trying* to tell you anything."

Tuck searched his brain for an explanation. "None of this makes sense."

"He was exhausted," said Amber. "Upset by—"

"Yeah, yeah. You've told me all that. But it's not credible. Dixon's a smart, solid, capable man."

Amber's voice rose. "You worked him into the ground."

"I didn't do a thing."

"Exactly," she said with finality.

He glared at her. "You're saying this is *my* fault?"

"Yes. Yours, your father's, Kassandra's, all of you."

He opened his mouth to defend himself, but no good argument formed inside his brain. Was it his fault? Why hadn't Dixon come to him? They could have talked. They could have worked things out. He'd have been happy to support his brother.

"Dixon is very private," Tuck explained to Amber.

"If I was you," she responded in a flat tone, "I'd stop worrying about why he went to Arizona. I'd worry about where he went from there."

She had a point. She had a very good point.

He pulled his phone from his shirt pocket and dialed Jackson.

"Hey" was Jackson's clipped answer.

"Dixon went to Arizona," said Tuck.

"You sure?"

"Scottsdale. A place called Highland Luminance. He

left there about five weeks ago, but we can pick up his trail. I'll meet you—" Tuck looked at Amber. "*We'll* meet you in Scottsdale."

Her eyes widened and she shook her head.

"I'm in LA," said Jackson. "I can be there in the morning."

"We'll be there tonight," said Tuck.

"No way," said Amber.

Tuck ended the call. "You obviously know my brother better than I do. You work for me again and I need you in Scottsdale."

"I really can't."

"Yes, you can." As far as Tuck was concerned, this was not negotiable.

Amber slipped quietly into Jade's hospital room, not wanting to disturb her if she was napping.

But she was sitting up in the bed reading a textbook, and she smiled. "Did you forget something?"

"No," Amber answered.

Jade wore a large yellow T-shirt and a pair of stretchy green pants visible though the open weave of her blanket.

"Is everything okay?" she asked.

"How are you feeling?"

"Good. I'm fine. But I'm feeling guilty just lying around here."

"You're studying." Amber rounded the bed, pulling a bright orange vinyl chair up closer.

"Not as hard as I should."

"That's okay. Your main job is to stay healthy and grow that baby for a few more weeks."

Jade's cheeks were rosy, her face puffier than usual, but her eyes looked clear and bright. She put a hand on her budging stomach. "The baby's getting bigger by the hour."

"That's what we want. I have some good news."

"I can go home?" Jade hesitated. "Well, to your home."

"No, you can't go home. Not yet. But I did get a job."

Jade started to smile, but for some reason she sobered, looking sad. "You're so good. You're amazing."

Amber wondered if her sister's hormones were messing with her mood. "It's just a job, Jade."

"No, it's not just a job." Jade looked like she might tear up.

"Hey." Amber reached for her sister's hand, worrying this might be a sign something was wrong. "What is it?"

Jade blinked. "It doesn't matter what I do, how much trouble I cause. You always take such good care of things."

"You're not causing trouble. I'm your big sister. Of course I'm going to help you."

Amber wished she didn't have to leave town right now. She knew Jade was an adult, and she knew the hospital would take good care of her. But she still felt guilty.

"Do you remember Earl Dwyer?" asked Jade.

The name took Amber by surprise. "You mean Mom's old boyfriend?"

Jade nodded, sniffing and dabbing at her nose with a tissue. She gazed for a moment at the reflection in the window. "I was thinking about him last night."

A picture of the man came up in Amber's mind and her neck prickled at the memory. "There's no reason to think about him."

"You remember how he yelled at us all the time?"

"You should be thinking happy thoughts for the baby."

"Do you remember?"

"Yes, I remember. But I'm surprised you do. You couldn't have been more than five when he moved out." Amber remembered Earl's snarling face, his booming voice and how she'd locked herself and Jade in their bedroom whenever an argument had started between him and their mother.

"I remember everything about him," said Jade, her voice going small.

Amber moved to the bed, perching on the edge to rub Jade's shoulder. "Well, stop. He's long gone."

"Do you remember the fire?" asked Jade.

"Yes." Amber couldn't figure out where Jade was going with this.

Was Jade worried about her own choices in men? Maybe she was worried about how her future boyfriends might impact her baby.

"Mom used to tell Earl not to smoke on the sofa," said Jade. "She yelled at him about it all the time. She said he was going to pass out, light the place on fire and kill us all."

"He nearly did." Amber shuddered at the memory of the acrid smell, the billowing smoke, the crackling flames rising from the sofa stuffing.

"That's how I knew it would work." Jade's eyes seemed unfocused.

"How what would work?"

"He passed out that night," said Jade, twisting her fingers through the blanket weave as she spoke. "Mom was in her bedroom. I remember Janis Joplin was playing on the radio." Jade sang a few bars. "You were asleep."

"So were you," said Amber.

But Jade shook her head. "I was awake. I went into the living room. I was so scared he'd wake up. I pictured it over and over, like an instant replay, those pale blue eyes opening, his stinky breath, his scabby hands grabbing me."

Amber went cold all over.

"But he didn't wake up," said Jade.

Amber let out a shuddering breath of relief.

"So I took his lit cigarette from the ashtray. I took the newspaper off the table. I crumpled a corner, just like I'd seen them do on that wilderness show. You remember? The one with the park ranger and the kids in Yellowstone?"

Amber couldn't answer.

"I tucked it all between the cushions, and I went back to bed."

"Oh, Jade," Amber rasped, her hand tightening on her sister's shoulder.

"I lit the fire, Amber." Tears formed in Jade's eyes. "I lit the fire and you put it out. It wasn't until years later that I realized I could have killed us all."

"You were five years old." Amber couldn't wrap her head around such a young child conceiving and executing that plan.

"Do you think I'm evil?"

"I think you were scared."

"I knew it would work," said Jade. "I knew if Earl set the sofa on fire that Mom would kick him out and we'd never have to see him again."

Amber drew Jade into her arms, remembering her as such a small child. "It was a fairly brilliant plan," she whispered against Jade's hair. "Another time, you might want to have a plan for putting the fire out."

"I was thinking last night," said Jade.

"You need to stop thinking about this. It's over."

"I was thinking that's how it's been my whole life. I've been starting fires, and you've been putting them out. And now I'm pregnant. And I'm sick."

"You're going to get better."

"But you have a new job. So my baby and I won't starve on the streets."

Amber's chest tightened painfully. "You're going to be just fine. We're *all* going to be just fine."

Jade's voice broke. "Thank you, Amber."

"You are so very welcome."

"I'm going to do better."

"You're already doing better."

"I'm going to get a job and I'm going to pay you back. And somehow, some way, I'm going to be the one helping you."

"Sure," said Amber. "But, for now, I have more good news."

Jade pulled away and looked up. "What more could there be?"

"I got a signing bonus. And it's enough to cover your hospital bill."

Jade blinked, her eyes clearing. "Are you kidding me?"

"I'm serious."

"Why? How? What's the job?"

Amber wasn't going to lie. "It's my old job."

It took Jade a moment to respond. "You're going back?"

"I'm going back."

Jade looked worried. "To Tuck? To the guy who kissed you?"

"To his brother. Dixon. Dixon will be back soon and I'll work for him again."

"He's the nice one, right?"

"He's the nice one." All Amber had to do was find him and get everything back to normal.

"What about Tuck?" asked Jade.

"What about him? He's barely ever there. Once Dixon's back, I'll never even have to see him."

Jade frowned. "But you kissed him."

"He kissed me."

"You kissed him back. I saw it. You kissed him back, which means you must be attracted to him."

Amber gave a shrug. "Maybe a little bit. He's a good-looking guy. And he's smart and funny. You should see the string of women lining up to date him. But nothing more is going to happen between us. He'll never really be interested in me."

She'd thought a lot about Tuck's kisses, concluding they were a power play, or a test like he'd said, or maybe it was just his habit to kiss any woman who happened to be around. If the tabloids were anything to go by, he did a lot of kissing with a lot of different women.

"You have to be careful of men," said Jade.

Amber didn't disagree, especially thinking about Earl and her mother's other boyfriends. Not to mention the stories about some of Jade's exes.

"Even when things start out well," said Jade, "they usually end badly."

Amber shifted from the bed back to the chair. "You and I agree on that."

"But lust is a funny thing."

"This isn't lust." Maybe it was curiosity, maybe sexual attraction, but what Amber felt for Tuck didn't rise to the level of lust.

"I've dated guys I knew were bad for me."

"You knew?"

"Yes, I knew. But it didn't keep me away. In fact it made them even more attractive."

"I'm not you," said Amber. She couldn't imagine herself setting aside good sense and taking up with a man who was clearly trouble.

Jade looked unconvinced.

"I have some other news," Amber said briskly, determined to move on. "I have to go away for a few days. It's for work."

Jade's eyes narrowed critically.

"For Dixon," Amber quickly added. She definitely didn't want Jade worrying about her. "He has a thing in Arizona, and I need to go out there. Do you think you'll be okay?"

"I'll be fine. I'm only going to lay here and study."

Amber congratulated herself on successfully switching the topic away from Tuck.

"Good." She came to her feet. "Because I have to leave tonight."

Jade's smile faded, but she gave a brave nod. "Are you sure you don't think I'm evil?"

Amber gave her sister a hug. "You're tough and brave, and a little bit brilliant. Take care of yourself. Feel good. And don't study too hard."

"Enjoy Arizona. Is Tuck going with you?"

Amber didn't have it in her to tell an outright lie. "Probably. For part of it anyway."

"Don't fall for him."

"I won't."

"He'll look sexy, and you'll want to. And I saw the way he looked at you. He wants to sleep with you."

An unwelcome wash of longing swept through Amber. "Too bad for him."

"Just say no."

"Well, I'm not going to say yes."

Amber wouldn't say yes. In fact, she doubted he'd ask again. He'd flat-out told her she wasn't as attractive as his usual dates.

Deep down inside, she knew she wasn't going to get another proposition from Tuck. He had far too many options in his life to even give her a second thought.

Seven

Tuck still wanted Amber. He wanted her very badly, and his desire was growing by the minute.

She was radiant in front of him, curled up in a padded rattan chair in the Scottsdale hotel courtyard. The gas fireplace flickering between them gave her face a gorgeous glow. Floodlights decorated the palm trees and rock garden behind her, while stars winked above them in the blackened sky.

"Do you have any ideas?" she asked.

There were any number of great ideas pinging around inside his head. But he doubted Amber was anywhere near his wavelength.

She was a picture of openness in a midnight blue knee-length dress and a cropped cardigan sweater with the sleeves pushed up. Her spiky sandals were dropped carelessly on the concrete patio in front of her. After her second glass of wine, she'd tugged her hair loose, and it flowed over her shoulders.

"I'm his brother," said Tuck, knowing she'd understand he was talking about their earlier conversation at Highland Luminance. "There must be someone who can authorize a release of information to me."

"The receptionist didn't seem encouraging." Amber referred to the woman who had asked them to leave the wellness resort.

"I can't imagine his yoga participation requires the same confidentiality rules as, say, an STD diagnosis."

"She did tell us the date he left."

"More than five weeks ago."

Amber took another sip of her wine, dark against her lush lips. Her face and shoulders were creamy and smooth. He remembered her taste, her scent and the feel of her lithe body enclosed in his arms.

"We should brainstorm about Dixon," she said.

Tuck shook himself out of a fantasy that had him kissing a shadow next to her collarbone. "What do you mean?"

"What do you know about him? Any unfulfilled dreams, secret desires?"

"He doesn't tell me his secret desires." Nor did Tuck confide in Dixon. And he was especially keeping quiet about his feelings for Amber.

"Toss out anything," she said. "What about when you were young, while you were growing up?"

"My desires have changed since I was young. I imagine his have, too."

"Play along," said Amber. "What else have we got to do?"

Tuck didn't dare voice his ideas.

The slight breeze rustled her hair and she brushed it back from her cheek. "Funny thing, I was reminded earlier today that childhood events can impact our entire lives."

He forced the sexy images from his mind. "You think Dixon is reacting to his childhood?"

"I think he's reacting to exhaustion and a cheating wife. But how he reacts could be influenced by his core self-perception."

"Core self-perception. Is that from the Highland Luminance brochure?"

"No." Her tone turned defensive. "It's from a documentary. But it's valid. It just means who you think you are."

"Who do you think you are, Amber? What's your core self-perception?" He was more interested in her than in Dixon.

"That's easy. I'm organized, a caretaker. I can't leave people to their own mistakes."

Tuck couldn't help but smile at the answer. "You left me to my own mistakes."

"Only after you fired me. Up until then, and against my own better judgment, I was helping you."

He knew that she had. "I was grateful."

"I could tell."

"I hired you back," he pointed out.

"Only because you needed me."

"True. But here you are."

"What about Dixon?"

"Don't you want to know about me?" Tuck knew the question sounded a bit needy, but he couldn't help himself.

"I already know your self-perception."

"Do tell."

"Talented, successful and good-looking. You know you're talented because so many things come easy, and the rest is reflected back in the mirror."

Her assessment was wholly unflattering.

"So I'm conceited?"

"I think you're singularly realistic."

"I was born into a rich family that had few expectations of me."

She didn't disagree.

"But that doesn't make me feel talented and successful," Tuck continued. "It makes me feel spoiled and useless."

Her expression turned decidedly skeptical. "Yet you don't do anything to change it."

He refused to argue. If she hadn't noticed how hard he'd been working lately, pointing it out to her wasn't going to change a thing.

"I'm here, aren't I?" he asked instead.

"To get back to the status quo."

"For the benefit of Tucker Transportation."

She seemed to consider that for a moment. "You're doing a pretty good job, you know."

At first he thought he must have misheard. "Excuse me?"

"You heard me. Don't fish for compliments."

"You took me by surprise with that."

She leaned slightly forward. "You're doing a pretty good job. This desperation to find Dixon is about you getting away again, not about the health of the company."

"You're wrong." Tuck might have been reluctant to come on board, but he was actually glad he had. He'd felt more useful in the past six weeks than ever had before in his life.

"I'm right," she said. "But we could go back and forth on it all night long."

Tuck bit back an all-night-long quip. He really had to get his craving for her under control.

"This is about Dixon," said Amber, her tone going crisp. "In the past, when he was young, what made him happy? What made him angry?"

"I made him angry," said Tuck.

She broke a grin at that. "Why does that not surprise me?"

"Because I'm the villain in this story."

"How did you make him angry?"

"I stole Nanny Susie's candies," he told her. "She kept a jar of them in the pantry as treats for good behavior. I dragged a kitchen chair into the pantry and piled a step stool on top, then I climbed up and filled my pockets. Dixon was freaking out. He was sure we'd be caught."

"That's bizarrely ironic."

"That I stole the good-behavior treats?" He grinned. "I get that now. I didn't get it then. They were delicious."

"Did you get caught?"

"No."

"Did Dixon eat the candies?"

"Yes. He held out for a while, but eventually he gave in. Maybe the experience scarred him? Should we be canvassing the local confectionaries?"

She rolled her eyes. "What else have you got?"

"I used to sneak out my bedroom window and meet girls in the middle of the night."

"Did Dixon sneak out with you?" she asked.

"No. By then, I guess he held firmer to his convictions. Or else he was loyal to his girlfriend. Which, now that I think about it, he really was. He only had two of them before Kassandra. Bettina Wright and Jodi Saunders. They were both gorgeous, but they also struck me as boring and a little stuck-up."

"You have different tastes than your brother."

Tuck let his gaze rest on Amber. "I do."

He knew that if he'd been working side by side with her for five years, married or not, his loyalty would absolutely have come into question.

The air seemed to thicken and heat between them. If he'd been closer, he'd have reached for her.

"So Dixon is dependable," Amber said into the silence. "He's honest, loyal and hardworking."

"You sound like my father."

"Even in the midst of an emotional crisis, first he tries to get your father's permission to leave. Then he leaves your father a letter of explanation and me as a fail-safe."

"You weren't much of a fail-safe."

"I told you I thought you could handle it. I still believe you could handle it if you'd apply yourself."

"Apply myself with no knowledge or experience to the running of a multinational conglomerate?"

"Whose fault is it that you have no experience?"

Tuck wanted to say his father's. He wanted to say his brother's. But he knew it was also his own fault. He'd sat back and allowed this to happen.

Had he always chosen the shortcut? Steal the candies instead of earning them? Make out with the girls without dating them?

"Do you think people can change?" he asked.

"I think we can try."

He felt the magnetic pull between them again.

Her expression turned guarded and she rose to her feet. "I should really go to bed."

He stood with her. "Any chance that's an invitation?"

"Tuck."

He immediately regretted the joke. "I know."

She looked up at him, eyes deep blue, cheeks flushed, the

breeze teasing her hair. Her lips were slightly parted and they looked so incredibly kissable.

"Is your flirting reflex really that strong?" she asked.

"It's not a reflex."

"Then, what is it?"

"It's you, Amber. It's all you."

"I'm not trying to send signals."

"You're not trying, but I know you feel it, too."

"Can you make it stop?" she asked, her voice a rasp.

He slowly slipped his arm around the small of her back, settling it there. "Why?"

She leaned slightly away, but she didn't break his hold. "Because it won't end well."

"We don't know that."

"One of us does."

"You can't predict the future."

"I can predict the next sixty seconds."

He gave a cautious smile. "I'm afraid to ask."

"You're going to kiss me, Tuck."

"That's a relief." He tightened his hold on her and leaned in. "I thought I was getting a knee to the groin."

"And then we'll—"

"Then nothing," he said. "Kissing you will take at least the next sixty seconds."

The sixty seconds passed, and then another and another. Tuck's lips were firm, his body taut and his embrace was sturdy and sure. The fire brought a glow to her skin, and the heat of passion built inside her.

She knew they had to stop. But she didn't want to stop. She didn't want to step away from the cradle of Tuck's arms or from the tendrils of desire weaving their way along her limbs. She decided she could risk a few more seconds, relish a few more moments of paradise.

They were both unattached, consenting adults. They could hug and kiss and generally test the limits of their endurance without bringing the world to a screeching halt. They were on a public patio, screened only by cactus plants and a latticework of vines. It wasn't as if things could get too far out of hand. Could they?

Tuck broke the kiss and dragged in a strangled breath. He buried his face in the crook of her neck. His palms slid lower, cupping her rear, pressing her into the V of his legs. His body was firm and aroused. The realization should have worried her rather than thrilling her.

"What happens next?" he asked between labored breaths.

She knew she had to get herself under control. It was time to say no, time to remind them both of who they were, time to politely retreat to her room and regroup for tomorrow.

"I thought I knew," she said instead.

"You don't?"

"I do," she said against his chest. "I should. I thought I did."

He drew back just far enough to look at her. "You're overthinking."

"I'm underthinking." If she was even contemplating letting things go further, she wasn't giving it anywhere near enough thought.

"That sounds promising."

"Tuck." She sighed, leaning against his strength for one last moment.

"I have a marvelous room," he responded, his voice rumbling deeply. "A huge bed, an enormous tiled shower and I bet room-service breakfast is fantastic. And I'm willing—no, *eager*—to share it all with you." But then his hold on her loosened and his tone changed. He drew back even farther. "But when a woman has to debate this long about whether or not to make love, the answer is already there."

She wanted to disagree. But he was right. And he was being such a gentleman about it.

It was chivalrous and admirable, and she was deeply disappointed. What had happened to the bold Tuck who'd stolen candies and sneaked out his bedroom window?

"You're saying no."

"I'm saying *hell yes.* But I don't want you to regret anything. And you would."

He was right again.

"You're nicer than people think," she said.

"I'm smarter than people think."

"Is this you being smart?"

"Responsible. This is me being Dixon. I've always known he was the better man."

"Yet you're here. And he's missing."

"Life is full of ironies."

She forced herself to take a step back, out of Tuck's embrace. "I'm really sorry."

He gave a self-deprecating shrug. "That you don't want to sleep with me?"

"That I let things get away from me. I didn't mean to lead you on."

"I'd rather have the shot than not." He reached out and smoothed her hair. "Kiss me any old time you like. And take it as far as you want. I can handle the disappointment. Who knows, maybe one day you'll be sure about what you want."

It was on the tip of her tongue to agree. But she didn't dare voice it. If she wasn't careful, she would convince herself she wanted him now, right now.

"Don't look so scared," he said.

"This isn't like me."

"It's called *chemistry*, Amber. It doesn't have to mean anything."

Her chest went hollow. Reality brought with it intense disappointment. "So you've felt this before? You've done this before?"

"All the time."

And it meant nothing to him. Good that they'd cleared that up. Jade was right. Getting involved with the wrong man inevitably ended badly.

"I'll never be sure." Then she realized it sounded as though she was waffling. "I mean, I'm already sure. The answer is no, and it's going to stay no. I'm here to work. I'm here to find Dixon. And that's all. Full stop."

"You want to add an exclamation point to that?"

"You're mocking me."

"I am. You have to admit, it was a quick turnaround."

"It took me a minute to get my head on straight. That's all. Good night, Tuck."

"Good night, Amber." The mocking tone was still in his voice.

She struggled to leave things on a professional note. "Jackson will be here in the morning?"

"You think Jackson will protect your virtue?"

"I'm thinking about finding Dixon. I've moved on."

She had. No more kissing Tuck. No more touching Tuck. No more flirting with Tuck.

She would keep her distance and keep it professional.

After a sleepless night fantasizing about Amber, and repeatedly asking himself why on earth he'd behaved like a gentleman, Tuck wasn't in the mood to care about corporate sales. But Lucas was on the phone asking, and Lucas was right. Robson Equipment was an important client and Tuck was only half an hour from Phoenix.

"Tell them yes," he said to Lucas. "Jackson showed up with a couple of guys. I'm sure they can spare me for a few hours."

Robson Equipment was hosting a black-tie business event and Lucas had arranged an invitation. It would be a chance to Tuck to touch base with the corporate brass and head off any moves Zachary Ingles might be making to poach the account.

"Take Amber," said Lucas.

"Jackson needs her help."

"Tell him he needs to share."

After her stance last night, Tuck couldn't imagine Amber agreeing to attend a dinner. "I don't need a date."

"She's not your date. She's your assistant. She knows the

account inside out and I'm beginning to think she's smarter than you."

"Ha-ha."

"That wasn't a joke."

"I doubt she'll agree," Tuck told him flat out.

"She's there to work, isn't she?"

Tuck didn't want to explain the complexity of their relationship, not that he was even sure how. The chemistry between them was combustible. He'd lied to her last night. What he'd felt with her didn't happen all the time. He'd never experienced anything like it in his life.

He could vow to keep his hands off her. But he was too smart to trust himself. He might have decided to behave more like Dixon, but it was definitely going to take some practice.

"Tuck?" Lucas prompted.

"She'll be working all day already."

"So pay her overtime."

"I'm not sure—"

"What did you do?"

"What do you mean?"

"You did something to upset her."

"I did not. Okay, I did. But it's not what you think."

"What do I think?"

"That I made a pass at her."

"That's exactly what I think. I bet she said no. And I hope you remember that for next time."

"She didn't say no. Far from it." Tuck checked his ego, but not quite in time.

There was a pause. "What did you do?"

"Nothing. But it's complicated."

"Uncomplicate it," said Lucas.

If only it was that easy. "You're such an armchair quarterback."

"Do I need to quote the Robson sales figures for last year?"

"No." Tuck knew they were significant.

"Are you going to argue that she doesn't know the portfolio?"

"I'm not." Tuck knew he was being cornered, but there wasn't a thing in the world he could do to stop it.

Lucas was right on all counts. Lucas was looking out for the best interests of Tucker Transportation, which is exactly what Tuck needed to be doing.

A knock sounded on the hotel room door.

"Get it done," said Lucas.

"I will."

"I'll talk to you after." Lucas ended the call.

Tuck finished buttoning his shirt as he crossed the living room of the suite. It was southwest in character, lots of rusts, browns and yellows, creating a warm atmosphere. The bed had been extraordinarily comfortable, the room temperature perfect with a fresh, fragrant breeze coming in from the desert side.

He'd returned here last night to find chilled champagne and chocolate-covered strawberries. Nice touch, but it was impossible to enjoy them by himself. He'd longed to invite Amber over to share, only to talk, just to listen to her voice, watch her expressions.

He blew out a cold chuckle as he reached the door. He wasn't kidding anyone, least of all himself. He wanted Amber in his bed, naked, smiling, welcoming him into her arms without a single mental reservation.

He answered to find her in the outdoor breezeway, Jackson by her side. Even without a smile, she was gorgeous, totally perfect.

"We've checked hospitals, morgues and police stations," said Jackson, heading directly into the room.

Tuck dragged his gaze away from Amber. "I take it you found nothing."

It wasn't a question. If there was bad news, Jackson's manner would be quite different.

"No leads from airlines, private or public. We've checked trains, buses and rental cars."

"Buses?" Tuck couldn't bring himself to believe Dixon would take a bus. "Have you *met* my brother?"

Amber marched into the room, expression schooled, her manner all business. He inhaled her subtle scent as she passed, feeling pathetic.

"He could have bought a car," she suggested.

"That would be more like him," Tuck agreed.

"We'll check to see if anything was registered in his name or in the company's. In case he stayed here in the Scottsdale area, we're also checking hotels, motels and resorts."

"Surely, he wouldn't buy a house," said Amber. She still hadn't looked directly at Tuck.

"Depends on how long he's planning to stay," said Tuck, willing her to meet his eyes.

"I suggest we have breakfast," said Jackson. "Then Amber and I will walk through everything she remembers."

"What about Highland Luminance?" Tuck asked.

"Their records are confidential."

"I know, but maybe you could—"

"Probably best if that's the last question you ask on that front," said Jackson.

"Got it." If Jackson was up to something less than legal, Tuck didn't want to know.

Amber looked puzzled. "What are you planning to—"

Both men shot her warning looks.

"Right," she said and shut up.

Tuck stuffed his wallet into his back pocket and located the room key. "Let's get started on what Amber remembers."

"It'll be better if she and I do it alone," said Jackson.

Tuck fought a spurt of jealousy. "No."

"She needs to be relaxed."

"She is relaxed. She will be relaxed."

"Given your history…" said Jackson.

Tuck couldn't believe she'd told him about last night. "Our *history*?" he challenged.

"You fired her."

"That?"

"Yes, that."

"I need to hear what she has to say," said Tuck.

"She doesn't want you there."

Tuck tried to catch her gaze again. He willed her to reassure Jackson, but she didn't.

"She might prompt a memory, remind me of something from our childhoods."

"You're going to use that against me?" Amber challenged.

"Do you or do you not believe Dixon's background might be relevant?"

Her blue eyes narrowed.

"It's not as if you're going to be naked."

"Oh, *that's* helpful," Jackson mocked.

"He's just being ridiculous," said Amber.

"She's right," Tuck agreed. "But I don't want to miss something because neither of you recognize its significance."

There was a beat of silence. "He's also right," said Amber, her shoulders dropping a notch.

Tuck would take the win.

"Don't gloat," she said to him.

"I'm not."

"You're such a liar." She started for the door.

"I'm going to need her tonight," Tuck said to Jackson.

Both Amber and Jackson swung their gazes his way.

"Robson Equipment is hosting a corporate event in Phoenix. Lucas said, and I'm quoting here, Amber has to attend because she's smarter than me, and we can't afford to lose the account."

"Fine by me," said Jackson.

Amber opened her mouth, but Tuck cut her off. "Double overtime. You'll be well compensated."

She hesitated. Then she nodded and turned for the door.

Tuck was surprised, shocked even. Money had swayed her again? This was starting to seem too easy.

Eight

Amber had dredged up every possible memory about Dixon's plans. Jackson was very good at his job, leading her down pathways that would have seemed insignificant to her, but clearly helped form the picture of Dixon's state of mind.

Tuck had been quiet throughout the conversation, excusing himself afterward without comment. She couldn't tell if he was pursuing a new lead or if he was annoyed with something she'd said. Jackson had immediately left to meet with his team, leaving Amber with some time to call Jade.

The news from the hospital was all good. Jade's blood pressure was stable and there were no other worrisome signs. They'd done an ultrasound and the baby still seemed fine. The technician had given odds on it being a girl.

Amber had also discovered that her signing bonus had been deposited into her bank account. It was a huge relief to know she was able to pay the hospital bills as they arrived.

Up next was the Robson party. After their kiss last night, she was nervous about spending the evening alone with Tuck. But she reminded herself that this was what she'd signed up for. Finding Dixon was one thing, but she also had to help Tuck keep the company running.

Lucas had said the Robson party would be formal—evening-gown and black-tie formal. She had a sleeveless, black crepe dress at home that would have worked. But she'd traveled light, with nothing but business and casual clothes in her suitcase.

Fingers mentally crossed, she navigated the hallway to the lobby shops, hoping the hotel boutique had something suitable.

She stopped at their display window, taking in a sublimely

beautiful cobalt blue dress. The cap sleeves were sheer netting and appliqué, with a fitted, crisscross bodice of supple, lightweight tulle. The dress was finished with an elegant, full skirt that glittered under the display lights.

It was perfect. It was also ten times Amber's price range.

She wandered inside, checking out the few formal gowns among an eclectic women's collection that ranged from hats and purses, to beachwear and jackets. She found a couple of dresses that would work without breaking her bank account and the saleslady directed her to a compact fitting room.

She started with an unadorned navy gown with three-quarter-length sleeves and a V-neck. It was neutral, and she could see how it would fit well on many body shapes. She moved out of the cubicle to look in the full-length mirror.

"A bit uninspiring," said a male voice behind her.

She turned to find Tuck, a plastic suit bag slung over his arm.

"Great minds think alike," he said, holding up what was obviously a newly purchased outfit for the evening.

She turned back to the mirror. "It's not bad. It's not as if I have a lot of choices."

"I do like the shoes."

Fortunately, Amber had tossed in a pair of silver spike heels that had just enough rhinestones to make them interesting. They weren't perfect with the navy dress, but she could get away with them.

"I've got a pair at home that would work better with this dress."

"I have no doubt that you do."

She peered at him in the mirror, trying to determine his level of sarcasm.

"Don't look so suspicious. Your extensive shoe collection is one of my favorite things about you."

"Nice save."

"It wasn't a save. I'm saying you need a different dress."

"There's not much to choose from."

He pointed over his shoulder at the display window. "What about that one?"

The saleslady was quick to pounce. "We do have it in her size."

"Great," said Tuck.

"Wrong," said Amber. She hated to be crass, but she didn't see any point in pretending. "It's too expensive."

"It's a business function," said Tuck.

"I know that."

"She'll try it on," he said to the saleslady.

"No, she won't."

"I'm not asking you to pay for it."

"You're sure not paying for it."

He was her boss, not her boyfriend. A few kisses notwithstanding, they didn't have the kind of relationship that allowed him to buy her clothes or anything else for that matter.

"Not me, Amber. Tucker Transportation."

"That's not how it works."

"That's exactly how it works. You're here on business. I'm compelling you to attend a *business* function. Your wardrobe is the company's responsibility."

"Did the company buy your suit?" she challenged.

"Yes."

"You're lying."

"Corporate credit card." There was a distinct note of triumph in his voice. He gestured to the navy dress. "You're not going in that."

"Yes, I am."

"Like it or not, Amber. Part of your function tonight is to be a billboard for Tucker Transportation's success."

She could barely believe he'd said it. "A *billboard*?"

"Don't get all high and mighty. It's part of the gig."

"You're saying I'm visual entertainment for your boardroom cronies? Do you want me to jump out of a cake, too?"

The saleslady had just returned with the dress and her mouth dropped open at Amber's jibe.

"It applies to me, as well," said Tuck. "Thanks." He smiled at the saleslady and took the dress from her arms. "I can't show up in a cheap suit."

"I don't imagine you own a cheap suit."

"Don't pretend you don't understand my point. You know full well what I mean. You and I both have to look the part tonight."

Amber hated that she did, but she got what he meant. And he wasn't wrong. She glanced at the rich cobalt blue dress. The irony was that it would be perfect with her shoes.

She looked for a graceful way forward. "Tell me this isn't the first time Tucker Transportation bought somebody a dress."

"This isn't the first time Tucker Transportation bought somebody a dress."

She gave him a skeptical frown.

"I think," he added. "Okay, I don't care. My rationale is sound." He glanced at his watch. "And we're running out of time. You might want to do something with your hair."

"What's wrong with my hair?"

The saleslady piped up. "We have a lovely salon in the hotel."

"Can you get her an appointment?" asked Tuck.

"Right away."

"This is ridiculous," Amber muttered. But she scooped the dress from Tuck.

It would be, by far, the most luxurious thing she'd ever worn. But if the man was determined to drop that much money for a single evening, who was she to fight him?

In the opulent ballroom, Tuck had to struggle to keep from staring at Amber. He'd expected the dress to transform her from her usual librarian look. But he'd had no idea the effect would be this dramatic.

The salon had styled her hair in an updo, wispy around her temples, showing off her graceful neck and highlighting her amazing cheekbones. Her makeup was subtle, but deeper and richer than she normally wore. Her thick, dark lashes and artfully lined eyes reflected the deep blue of her dress.

At the moment, he was trying hard to concentrate on Norm Oliphant's description of his newly evolving supply chain, but he was torn between watching Amber and glaring at the dozens of men checking her out. Didn't they realize she was with him?

Dinner was over and a music ensemble was filing into the room. Lighting was being subtly adjusted, dimmed around the perimeter, slightly brighter to highlight the polished wood dance floor.

"I hope there's some good news about your father," said Norm.

Tuck checked his wandering mind and told himself to behave like Dixon. Kassandra had been gorgeous as well, but he was certain his brother had never let that detract from business discussions.

"We're all encouraged," Tuck said to Norm.

"So you've seen him recently?" asked Norm's wife, Regina.

Tuck wasn't sure how to answer that. Truth was he hadn't seen his father since they'd move him to Boston. But how was that going to sound?

Amber smoothly and unexpectedly stepped in. "Tuck has become so pivotal to the day-to-day operations, Jamison is insistent that he focus on the company. Jamison has his wife with him, of course. She's been a stalwart support every day during his recovery. But he gathers peace of mind knowing Tuck is at the helm."

Tuck could have cheered. It was all lies, of course, made up on the spot, which made her explanation all the more impressive.

"Where's Dixon in all of this?" asked Norm.

Amber stepped slightly closer to both Norm and Regina, lowering her voice, throwing Norm off balance with the intensity of her gaze. "I'm sure you heard what happened. With Dixon's wife?"

"We did," said Regina, leaning in.

Amber nodded. "Tuck insisted Dixon take some time to himself. He left a contact number, but we haven't wanted to bother him. You know how brothers can be when one is betrayed. They value loyalty above everything."

Regina glanced at her husband.

"Loyalty," Norm agreed with a nod.

"In business as well as life," said Amber.

Her words were bang on, the inflection perfect. Tuck had to glance at her to convince himself she'd done it on purpose.

He caught her gaze and realized she had. She had skillfully and adroitly reminded Norm of his long-standing business arrangement with Tucker Transportation. She was frighteningly good at this.

Then Amber gave the man a dazzling smile.

Norm raised his glass to Tuck in a toast. "Good of you to come tonight."

"Good of you to invite us." Tuck took a drink with him.

The small orchestra came up with opening bars on the opposite side of the hall.

"We'll be in touch next week," Norm said to Tuck. "I hear Zachary Ingles moved on."

"I'm afraid he thought the grass was greener," Tuck said with a disapproving frown, deciding to stick with the loyalty theme.

"Don't like to see that," said Norm.

"I've promoted Lucas Steele to vice president. Good man. He's been with us for over a decade."

"Worked his way up through the ranks?" asked Norm, looking pleased by the notion.

"Absolutely," said Tuck, though he had no idea exactly how far through the ranks Lucas had worked his way up. "Corporately, we like to nurture talent."

Tuck was tossing things out on the fly, but it seemed like a vague enough statement to be true of most companies.

"Have Lucas give my guys a call," said Norm.

"First thing Monday," said Tuck.

Norm smiled at Regina. "Shall we dance, dear?"

"My pleasure, darling."

Tuck and Amber watched the two walk away.

"You were good," she said. "Very confident, very much in charge."

"Me? You're the one who deserves an acting award. My father gathers peace of mind knowing I'm in charge?"

"I'm sure he does. Or he would. If he knew what I know."

Tuck arched a brow. "Dixon left a contact number?"

She gave a sly smile. "He did. It didn't work in the end, but he did leave a number."

"Remind me to listen very carefully to how you phrase things."

"You don't already?"

Tuck started to smile, but then he caught another man eyeing Amber and sent him a withering stare.

"We should dance," he said.

"Why?"

Because she might not be his date, but she'd arrived with him. He wasn't used to having women poached from under his nose, and he wasn't about to start now.

"It'll look good," he said, taking her hand.

"To who?" But she came easily as he started walking.

"Norm and Regina."

"You think?"

"Sure."

Why wouldn't it look good? It was a perfectly acceptable excuse. They made it to the dance floor and Tuck turned her into his arms.

She fit perfectly. Of course she fit perfectly. And she smoothly matched his rhythm. Within seconds, it was as if they'd been dancing together for years. He immediately relaxed, drawing her closer.

"Thank you for all that," he said into the intimacy of their embrace.

"Just doing my job."

"You're doing it extraordinarily well."

"I guess that's what you get when you pay double overtime."

Tuck smiled at that. "You're a mercenary at heart."

She was quiet for a moment. "Money makes life easier."

"It can," he agreed. "But it can also be a burden."

Right now, Tuck felt the weight of every employee who depended on Tucker Transportation.

Her tone turned teasing. "Spoken like a man who just spent a mortgage payment on a dress."

"In order to ensure hundreds of other people can make their next mortgage payment."

"Do you have any idea how that feels?" she asked.

"To make a mortgage payment?" He wouldn't pretend he did. "The house has been in our family for a couple of generations."

"To worry about making your mortgage payment. To worry about paying for food, clothes, medical bills."

"You know I don't."

They danced in silence. He could tell she was annoyed with him. He didn't really blame her. From the outside looking in, his life must seem like a walk in the park.

Then it hit him, what she might be saying.

"Do *you* earn enough money?" he asked.

She glanced up in obvious surprise. "What?"

"Should I give you a raise?"

"Where did that come from?"

"It sounded as though you were having money problems."

"You pay me fairly."

He searched her expression. He could tell the conversation was hitting very close to home for her. If it wasn't now, then when? When had she been worried about meeting expenses?

"Your childhood?" he suggested.

"This isn't about me."

"Your childhood?" he repeated.

"Fine. We were poor. My mom was single. She drank. A lot."

He digested the information. "I'm sorry you had to go through that."

The orchestra switched songs, but he kept on dancing.

"It was a long time ago," said Amber. "Truth is, it impacted Jade more than it impacted me."

"How so?"

"She had a hard time settling into life. She quit school, left town. Then she bounced from job to job. She always picked the wrong men."

Interesting, but Tuck was far more curious about Amber than he was about Jade. "And you? Did you pick the wrong men?"

She gave a little laugh. "I didn't pick any men at all. Well, not many. I had a boyfriend in high school. But then I graduated and started working. I took a lot of night-school courses at community college, so there wasn't much time for a social life."

"You don't date?" Tuck couldn't help but contrast his own active social life.

"Occasionally. Casually." She glanced around the opulent ballroom. "I have to say, this is the most extravagant event I've ever attended. I guess I should thank you for the experience."

"Anytime." He was serious.

His brain ticked through the information she'd just given him. He liked the idea of what he thought she had to mean.

"So you're saying..." He tried to frame the question. "How do I put this..."

"Don't you *dare* ask me about my sex life."

As if anything on earth would stop him. "Tell me about your sex life."

"Shut up."

He gave a brief chuckle. "I'll tell you about mine."

"I've read about yours."

"Not the details."

"Nobody wants the details."

"I disagree. Reporters ask me about them all the time." He maneuvered them around the crowd to a quieter spot on the dance floor.

"Do you answer?"

"No. If I did, they'd be disappointed."

"Did you just tell me you're a bad lover?"

"What? No. I meant that I'm not as practiced as people assume." He hesitated, then went for it. "Not that you'd have a basis for comparison."

"You're outrageous." But her tone was laced with amusement.

"I won't argue with that. But I'm also available. You know, if you're in dire need of—"

The end of her fist connected sharply with his shoulder, startling him.

"Ouch."

"You better believe, *ouch*," she sniffed with mock offense. "I had a boyfriend."

"Not since high school."

"And I've had offers since then."

He knew that was true. "At least a dozen tonight alone."

She looked puzzled.

"You're not paying attention, are you?" he asked.

"To what?"

"To all the men in the room eyeing you up."

She seemed surprised. "It's the dress. And maybe the hair. Probably the shoes."

"It's all of that," he agreed. "But it's more than just that."

He couldn't help himself. He splayed his hand across her back, urging her close, molding their bodies together.

"Tuck."

"I won't pretend I'm not attracted to you."

The word *attracted* was the understatement of the century. He was wild about her, burning hot for her, growing more so by the hour.

"Jackson's here."

It took a moment for her words to make sense. He'd pictured their conversation taking an entirely different turn.

She signaled the direction with a nod and Tuck easily spotted Jackson in the crowd. He stood out in blue jeans, a white T-shirt and a worn leather jacket. It was easy to tell from his expression that he had some news.

Tuck quickly escorted Amber from the dance floor, meeting up with Jackson at the edge. The three of them made for the double doors that led to a quiet foyer.

"Dixon bought a car," said Jackson when they emerged into the relative privacy of the long, high-ceilinged, glass-walled room.

"When?" asked Tuck.

"Five weeks ago, a three-year-old Audi convertible. He paid cash."

"Is he still in Scottsdale?"

"Didn't stay here long," said Jackson. "We tracked the car to a marina in San Diego."

Tuck's anticipation rose. "Did you find Dixon?"

"There, he bought a sailboat."

Tuck waited for Jackson to elaborate.

"Forty-footer. Paid cash."

The situation was getting stranger by the second.

"I thought you were watching his bank accounts," said Tuck.

"We are. Does your brother normally carry that kind of walking-around money?"

Tuck didn't know. But that did seem like a lot of money to have at his fingertips. How long had Dixon planned this little adventure?

"Did you find the sailboat?" asked Amber.

"It left the marina weeks ago and hasn't been back."

They all stared at each other in silence.

"I doubt he sank," said Tuck. "There'd have been a distress call. We'd have heard from the authorities by now."

"Probably," said Jackson.

"Was it equipped to sail solo?"

"It was."

"Something's not right," said Amber.

"No kidding," Tuck agreed. There were plenty of things not right in this.

"When he headed for Scottsdale," she said, "even though it was a secret, he left a letter for your dad, and he left a number with me. He was that careful. There's no way he'd sail off into the Pacific without telling anyone at all."

"That's exactly what he did," said Tuck.

His worry about his brother was rapidly turning to annoyance. What had Dixon been thinking?

Amber was shaking her head. "Not without any word at all. I can understand that he didn't like it at Highland Luminance. And clearly he can afford a nice boat. But he's not irresponsible. He's trying to clear his head so he can do a good job at Tucker Transportation. He's not trying to harm it."

"Trying or not," said Tuck, "that's exactly what he's doing." He really wished Amber would stop defending Dixon.

"He..." She snapped her fingers. "That's it."

"What's it?" asked Tuck.

"Jamison," she said. "Dixon would have contacted Jamison. He didn't know anything about the heart attack. As far as he's concerned, your dad's still running the company. We searched through Dixon's accounts. And we've been monitoring Jamison's work email, but not his personal email."

Jackson swore under his breath. He was instantly on his phone giving instructions to one of his staff.

Tuck had to admit it was possible. It was even likely. It certainly made more sense than anything else right now. For weeks now, Dixon could have been operating under the assumption they knew his plans. He thought Jamison was running the show. He had no idea Tuck was making a mess of it.

Dixon was still gone. And Tuck still had to find him. But at least it made a little bit of sense now.

* * *

It was late into the night, and the three of them were back in Tuck's hotel suite when Jackson received a copy of an email from his investigator. The original had been sent by Dixon to Jamison's little-used personal email address. Amber was relieved they'd found an answer and happy there was a logical explanation for Dixon's behavior.

"It was sent from an internet café the day he left San Diego," said Jackson from where he was sitting at the round dining table. "He says he plans to spend a few weeks sailing down the Pacific coast. He apologizes but tells your dad to have confidence in you. He knows you can do it."

Tuck shook his head. "Not under these circumstances."

He'd parked himself in an armchair beside the flickering gas fireplace.

Amber had chosen the sofa. She'd kicked the shoes off her sore feet and curled them beneath her. The cushions were soft under her body, while the heat from the fire warmed her skin. Her brain had turned lethargic at the end of such a long day and she would have loved to let herself fall asleep.

"Can you answer Dixon's email?" Tuck asked Jackson.

"Easy. But he'll have to stop somewhere and log on in order to see it."

"He might not check," said Amber. "The point of the whole exercise was to get away from everything."

"He's been away from everything," said Tuck. "It's time for him to come back."

"Before he's ready?" she asked. She understood Tuck's frustration, but Dixon had a right to take some time to himself.

Tuck sat up straight and his voice rose. "How much time does the guy need?"

"You tell me." Her annoyance gave her a renewed shot of energy. "You're the expert. You've had nothing but time to yourself for years now."

He frowned. "Not by choice."

"They held a gun to your head?"

Jackson rose, closing his laptop. He muttered something about having work to do as he headed for the suite door.

Tuck didn't react to him leaving. His attention remained focused on Amber. "They did everything possible to keep me at arm's length."

She found that hard to believe.

"You think I'm lying," he stated.

"I know you had an office. You had keys to the building. Dixon invited you to meetings."

"Meetings where my father took great pleasure in setting me up for failure."

"How?"

"By cornering me with arcane questions to prove I didn't know anything."

"*Did* you know anything?"

He glared at her and she regretted the question.

"I mean," she said, attempting to backtrack, "you could have studied up, surprised him, turned the tables on him."

"That seemed like a lot of work to impress a guy who only wanted me gone."

"Why would he want you gone?" Tuck might be a bit of a rebel, but what father wouldn't be proud to have him as a son?

"Because he liked Dixon better. Parents aren't all perfect, Amber. They don't automatically love their children."

"Your father loves you."

Even as she uttered the statement, Amber realized she had no idea how Jamison felt about Tuck. She was under no illusions about automatic parental love.

She shook her head, regretting her words. "I'm sorry. I don't know that. I don't know anything about it."

Tuck blew out a breath. "It's okay."

She gave a little laugh. "I don't even know whether my own mother loved me."

His gaze turned sympathetic.

Uncomfortable, Amber sat up a bit straighter, attempting to explain. "I'm not sure my mother knew how to love anyone.

She said she loved us. I even think she wanted to love us. But she was so incredibly self-absorbed, she couldn't see past her own needs and desires."

"And your father?"

"Long gone before I had any memory of him."

"Did he support you at all? Financially?"

Amber couldn't help but cough out a laugh. "I'd be surprised if he stayed out of jail. My mother had extraordinarily bad taste in men."

"Where is she now?"

"She died. It happened while Jade and I were still teenagers."

Deeper sympathy came up in Tuck's eyes, softening his expression, making him look approachable, sexy. This was not good.

"How are we talking about me?" she asked.

They needed to get back to arguing.

"You helped raise your sister?"

"She was sixteen when it happened. I was eighteen. There wasn't much raising left to do." And by that time there hadn't been much of an opportunity to change any of Jade's habits.

"That's when she dropped out of school?" he asked.

"She took off after a few months. I didn't hear from her for a while."

Tuck rose and helped himself to a bottle of water, holding one out for her.

She nodded and accepted it.

He sat down at the opposite end of the sofa. "What did you do?"

"I graduated from high school and got a job." She twisted the cap and broke the seal. "With Dixon. He took a chance on me."

"That's surprising," said Tuck.

"I worked hard. I promised him I would, and I did."

"I believe you." Tuck stretched one arm along the back of the sofa. "No wonder you have no patience for me."

"I wouldn't say—"

"It's way too late to protest now. From where you're sitting, I had it all, every advantage, every privilege. My education was paid for, and I walked straight into a VP job in Daddy's company."

"I've never complained about my employment." She'd been grateful for it. "Well, up until you fired me anyway."

"You're back."

"I am."

He seemed to ponder for a moment. "You think I squandered my birthright."

"Those are your words, not mine."

"Then, give me your words."

She took a minute to come up with an answer. "I think you've always had a lot of options. And most of them were very pleasant options. It's not hard to understand why you'd choose the easiest path."

"Ouch."

"Who wouldn't?"

"Apparently not you."

"That's because I never had any easy options." The memories of her teenage years brought a knot to Amber's stomach. "I could work my butt off and only just get by, or I could give up and spiral down like my mother."

She took a drink, letting the cool water bathe her throat.

"Some might say spiraling down would be the easy path," said Tuck.

"To a point. But after a while, it gets a whole lot harder." The thought of living like her mother—the drinking, the smoking, crappy housing, used clothes, the carousel of shabby men—made her physically ill. She took another sip.

"What would you do?" he asked. "If you were me? If you had what I have?"

"I'm not trying to tell you that I'm morally superior."

"What would you do?"

Her instinct was to continue arguing the point. But instead, she considered the theoretical question. "Then or now?"

"Then. No, hindsight is too easy. Now. What would you do now?"

"If I were you," she said. "I'd go home. I'd leave Dixon alone, and I'd go home, work hard and prove to my father that he was dead wrong."

"Because that's the hardest path?"

"Because that's the most satisfying path."

Tuck stared into her eyes for a long time.

She grew uncomfortable, worrying she'd made him angry.

"Will you help me?" he asked.

The question surprised her. But there was only one possible answer. And she meant it sincerely. "I will."

"Will you like me?" As soon as he'd uttered the words, he looked away. But he wasn't fast enough to hide the uncertainty in his eyes.

She realized he'd made himself uncharacteristically vulnerable with the question. She knew she had to be honest. "I already like you."

His posture seemed to relax. "You're one in a million, Amber."

He couldn't be more wrong about that.

"I'm incredibly average," she said. "Thing is, in your world, you don't often come across incredibly average."

A knowing smile came across his face. "Stand up."

The request was abrupt and she wondered what she'd done wrong. Did he want her to leave? He didn't look angry. But then, it was getting late.

She stood.

"Put on your shoes."

She slipped her feet into the delicate high heels. But as she made to head for the door, he gently grasped her shoulders, turning her away, propelling her in the opposite direction.

"What are you doing?"

Before he answered, they were through a set of open double doors and into the bedroom.

"Look," he said, turning her toward a full-length mirror.

"What?"

There was nothing to see. The dress still looked great and it still went with the shoes. But her hair was coming loose and her makeup had faded. Her cheeks were rosy from the earlier wine and maybe from debating with Tuck. Her eyes were slightly shadowed with exhaustion. She really did need to get some sleep.

He brushed his fingertips across her shoulder, his tone going deep. "Is there anything about you that is remotely average?"

His words sent a tingle down her spine.

"You're amazing, Amber. You're flat-out amazing. You're gorgeous and smart as a whip. You're insightful and funny." He brushed her hair from the side of her neck. "And I can't get you out of my mind."

He eased slowly forward until his lips connected with the crook of her neck. They were soft and hot as she gazed at his image in the mirror. He kissed her again, lips wider this time, leaving a circle of moisture behind.

He planted a chain of kisses along her shoulder while his palms slipped down her bare arms. She watched his dark head, felt the air cool the moisture on her skin, let desire and arousal throb to life inside her. Then his hands came to rest on her waist, his blunt fingers splayed on her stomach, dark in relief against the glittery blue of the dress.

She leaned back against him. He was solid, a tower of muscle and strength. Their gazes met in the reflection, midnight blue and pewter gray. She let him in, not flinching, absorbing his obvious passion and returning it with her own.

He reached for the zipper at the back of her dress, watching her reaction closely as he drew it down. The air brushed her back and she quivered with the mix of sensations. He brushed aside the fabric and kissed her shoulder. His fingers delved into her hair, tugging at the clip and releasing thick waves.

She gasped in a breath and her hands curled into fists. It was the point of no return. No, it wasn't. She'd already passed no return when she'd met his eyes in the mirror. Her and Tuck, for now, at least for this small moment, were inevitable.

She shrugged her shoulders and the dress slipped down, the fabric cascading over her breasts, past her hips, pooling on the thick carpet.

His eyes darkened, his gaze pausing on her pink satin bra. It swept over her navel to the tiny matching panties, down the length of her legs to the sparkling shoes.

"One in a million," he whispered in her ear.

His hand closed over her breast and he kissed that first spot on her neck.

She knew she should look away, close her eyes and safely drown in the sensations of his touch. But she watched while he unhooked her bra. He set her breasts tumbling free. Then he let his fingertips roam from the curve of her hip, to the indentation of her naval, to the mound of her breast and her pearled nipples.

He touched and fondled while her temperature rose and her lungs dragged in air. When his hand dipped under her panties, urgency overwhelmed her. She turned in his arms, meeting his lips, tangling her limbs around him while his hand drove her to heights of passion.

"You are incredible," he rasped between kisses, peeling off the flimsy panties.

She pushed off his jacket, then struggled with his tie.

He tore off the new shirt and they came together, skin on skin, finally. He embraced her, held her tight, strong arms wrapped firmly around her as he explored every nuance of her mouth.

Then he lifted her and carried her to the big bed, yanking back the covers to deposit her on the crisp sheets. She lay on her back, watching as he stripped off his clothes.

When he was naked, he gazed down. He took in her disheveled hair, his eyes moving over her breasts to the shadow of her thighs, down the length of her legs. Then he smiled.

She realized she still wore her shoes.

She couldn't help but grin sheepishly in return.

"One of the things I love best about you," he said, coming to lie next to her on the mattress.

He renewed his exploration of her body, and she returned the favor, reveling in the taut muscles of his shoulders and arms, his washboard stomach and the strength of his hips and thighs. She kissed her way over his salty skin while he found her sensitive and erotic spots, the crook of her knee, the inside of her thigh, the tips of her nipples.

Then he rolled on top, his solid weight pinning her satisfyingly to the mattress. He took a second with a condom, then stared straight in her eyes.

She flexed her hips upward and felt him sliding inside. Her head tipped back and her eyes fluttered closed. Her world contracted to the cloud of sensation that was Tuck. His scent surrounded her. His heat enveloped her. His fingertips were magic and his lips were delicious.

His rhythm was slow and steady. First her bones melted to nothing. Then her limbs began to buzz. His pace increased and she couldn't contain her moans. Wave after wave of passion washed over and through her.

She couldn't move. She couldn't breathe. Her mind had gone into a free fall. And then the world burst open, and she cried out his name, hanging on tight, never wanting to let go.

Nine

Tuck knew that making love couldn't have been an easy decision for Amber. But for him it had been the easiest path, and definitely the most pleasurable path.

He eased onto his side, taking his weight from her and gathering her close. "I'm sorry," he whispered.

"For?" she whispered back. "Was that not your best work?"

He wanted to laugh, but he was afraid it would be the wrong reaction. "I know you weren't sure."

She turned her head and looked questioningly up at him.

"About making love," he elaborated.

"Did I not seem sure?"

"I guess you did."

"Should I have made you wait?"

"That might have killed me. I've been desperate for you since day one."

She smoothed her hand across his chest. "I've been resisting you for a while now."

He let his ego absorb the compliment.

She curled herself into a sitting position.

"What are you doing?" He wanted her to stay exactly where she was.

She moved to the edge of the bed. "Now that we've got that out of our system."

"Whoa, what?" His system was just getting started.

She rose and crossed the bedroom. "I realize it was inevitable. It might be nothing but chemistry, but it's still pretty powerful stuff."

Nothing but chemistry?

Okay, sure, he remembered saying that. Problem was he couldn't remember why.

She slipped into her panties, turning to face him while she dressed.

For some reason, he'd expected her to be shy. He wasn't sure why, maybe because of the clothes she usually wore.

He sat up, draping his legs over the edge of the bed. "You don't have to leave."

She stopped in the midst of fastening her bra, looking surprised. "We need to get to sleep. I assume we'll be leaving first thing in the morning."

"There's no rush."

They were flying in a Tucker jet. They could leave any old time they wanted. It didn't even have to be tomorrow.

"We've got a ton of work to do," she said. "I said I'd help, and I will. I'll do as much as I can. But you've got to do your part, Tuck. Dixon could be back soon. You might not have much time and you need to start proving yourself."

Wait a minute. "We *want* Dixon back."

"Sure we do. But not right away, not if you want to show your father you've got what it takes to run the company."

Tuck came to his feet. "I don't have what it takes to run the company."

Amber dropped the dress over her head, pushing her arms through the flimsy cap sleeves. "Maybe not yet."

"I don't know what you think I can do."

"You can start by hiring some new executives. Lucas needs help." She turned and presented him with the zipper.

He didn't want to zip her up. He wanted to strip her down again. He wanted her naked again, in his bed, in his arms, making love until neither of them could move and then sleeping until noon.

"I can't hire new executives."

"Zip me up. Yes, you can."

"That's a permanent decision. I'm temporary."

"You're a Tucker and you're in charge. Make a decision."

This was the first time Amber had struck him as being cavalier. She was normally careful and methodical.

"Is there something wrong with my zipper?" she asked.

"You don't have to go yet."

She reached back and zipped herself, making it most of the way up. Then she turned and gave him a quick kiss. "I'm exhausted."

"Sleep here."

She stilled, a stricken expression crossing her face. Just as quickly, it disappeared. "That's not going to happen."

"Why not?"

"This was a bad idea. I mean, it was a good idea, because it had to happen. But at its foundation, it was a terrible idea. We need to forget about it and move on."

"Move on to *what*?"

He didn't want to forget about what had just happened between them. It was the greatest sex of his life.

"Haven't you been paying attention?" she asked. "You're going to run Tucker Transportation. It goes without saying, but I'm saying it anyway, absolutely no good can come from a fling between us. It'll compromise your credibility and it'll destroy my career. You've fired me once. I'm not about to give you or Dixon or your father a reason to fire me again."

"Nobody's going to fire you."

She shook her head. "That's the *only* sure thing that happens when assistants get involved with their bosses."

"You can't know that."

She took a deep breath, squaring her shoulders. "Do you want to do this?"

He didn't dare hope she meant make love again. "Do what?"

"Do you want to *try*? Or do you want to spend the rest of your life as a self-indulgent playboy and a vice president in name only?"

"Those are my only two choices?"

"Yes."

"Then, I'm willing to try."

At least he could still spend time with her. And maybe he could manage to impress her. And maybe, if he was very lucky, their chemistry would rear its head again and she'd come back into his arms.

In the breezeway outside Tuck's hotel suite, Amber sagged against the wall. It had taken everything she had to pull off the act, to pretend that making love with Tuck hadn't thrown her for an absolute emotional loop.

She might not have been able to stop herself. But she knew she'd made one of the world's biggest mistakes. She had hopped into bed with her boss. She'd hopped into bed with her boss, and it was fantastic.

At least it had been fantastic for her. Who knew what it was for him? Maybe he had sex like that every Saturday night.

Maybe she'd been mediocre. Maybe he'd been disappointed. She forcibly stopped her brain from going there.

She wasn't going to do that to herself. If it hadn't been good for him, too darn bad. He'd have to get past it, maybe move on to someone else. She was moving on. She was definitely moving on.

She straightened from the wall, putting one foot in front of the other. Her room was along the courtyard and up one flight of stairs. She was going to shower and sleep, and then she was going back home to focus on Jade, the baby and Tucker Transportation.

Tonight was a lark. It didn't have to define her. It didn't even need to define her relationship with Tuck.

"Amber?" Jackson's voice came from a pathway at a right angle.

She stopped. Her heart sank and her stomach contracted into a knot of embarrassment and guilt.

She forced herself to turn and face him. "Hello, Jackson."

"I'm glad I caught you." His expression wasn't condemning, nor was it judgmental.

Maybe he hadn't guessed what had just happened.

She should play it cool. She could have taken her hair down for any number of reasons. From this angle, he couldn't see her zipper was partway down. She made a mental note to keep her back away from him.

"Did Dixon ever mention a woman?" he asked.

Amber forced herself to stay calm and collected. "What kind of a woman?"

She fought off the urge to smooth her hair. It would only call attention to the mess.

"Someone other than Kassandra."

"You mean a girlfriend?" She knew that wasn't possible.

"Yes."

"Dixon wasn't fooling around. He was as honorable as they come."

"I know you're loyal to him."

"That's not loyalty talking," said Amber. "Jackson, he didn't cheat on Kassandra."

"What about after they separated?"

"Nobody I ever heard about."

Jackson showed her his phone with a photo of a pretty blond woman. "Recognize her?"

"No. Who is she?"

"Is there any chance, any chance at all, that Dixon left Chicago to be with another woman?"

"He wouldn't leave Chicago to do that. His friends would be cheering from the rooftops. He wouldn't hide it."

Jackson was obviously deep in thought.

"What's going on?" she asked.

"I'm covering all the bases."

"Where did you get the picture?"

"She might be connected to the sailboat. We're tracking it down the coast."

"There might not be so much of a rush now."

Amber was warming up to the idea of Tuck proving himself to his father. He'd obviously spent his whole life riddled with self-doubt. She knew he'd feel good if he succeeded. And she knew he had it in him. He just had to apply himself.

Jackson's brow rose. "Why do you say that?"

"Tuck's going to run the company. It's the first chance he's ever had. This might even turn out to be a blessing in disguise."

Jackson didn't respond, but skepticism came into his eyes.

"You think it's a bad idea." She wished she hadn't come to respect Jackson's opinion.

"I think it's not Tuck's idea."

"It was. Kind of." She struggled to remember the exact details of the conversation. "He's always felt inadequate."

Jackson looked amused. "He's been too busy having fun to feel inadequate."

"You're wrong."

"You've known him how long?"

"A few weeks," she admitted.

Jackson gave her an indulgent smile. "He's not what you think he is."

"Don't patronize me."

"Then, let me put it another way. He's not what you want him to be." Jackson's sharp eyes took in her messy hair and what had to be smeared makeup.

In that second, she knew she was caught. And it was humiliating. Jackson thought she was going after Tuck. He thought she wanted to domesticate Tuck. She could only imagine he thought she was one of a long line of gold diggers out to become Mrs. Tuck Tucker.

She had to get out of here. "Good night, Jackson."

"I like you, Amber."

She gave a chopped laugh of disbelief.

"You're too good for him," said Jackson.

"I don't want him."

Jackson's smile was indulgent again. "You want him to be a better him."

She opened her mouth to deny it.

But Jackson spoke overtop her. "There's only one reason a woman wants that."

"There could be a hundred reasons why a woman wants that."

"You might not know it yet. But you're falling for him. Don't fall for him, Amber. You'll only get hurt."

"Advice to the lovelorn, Jackson?"

"Advice from a guy who knows Tuck."

"Well..." She had no good comeback to that. She truly didn't know what to say. All she knew was that she wanted the heck out of this conversation right now. "Thank you."

She turned sharply away, then realized he'd seen her partially undone zipper.

She swallowed. She lifted her chin and squared her shoulders. He'd obviously already guessed. He'd come to all the wrong conclusions afterward, but he knew full well that she'd just slept with Tuck.

When she looked up and saw Amber, Jade closed her textbook and pushed the wheeled bed tray off to one side. "Welcome back to the real world."

"I'm on my way to the office," Amber told her, moving closer. "We landed about an hour ago."

Taking a private jet to Scottsdale and back had been a surreal experience for Amber, but there was no disputing the convenience.

"How was it?" asked Jade with enthusiasm. "Warm? Great? I looked up the resort—*nice*."

"We were pretty busy working." Amber had struggled all night long, then especially during the flight back, to keep focused on the work and not to think about Tuck.

Jade gave a mock frown. "You didn't spend hours at the spa?"

"I'm afraid not."

"I was hoping to live vicariously through you."

"I could lie," Amber offered.

"Would you? That would be nice. I'm so bloated and tired and achy, I'd kill for a massage or a few hours in the hot springs."

"The weather was great," said Amber. "The hotel was gorgeous, the food, rooms. The beds were really comfortable."

"Was that a Freudian slip?"

Amber didn't understand Jade's point.

"Beds," Jade elaborated. "Plural?"

Amber realized it was a joke, but embarrassment made her mind go momentarily blank.

Jade's eyes went wide. "Wait a minute."

"It was a figure of speech," said Amber.

Jade's surprise turned to concern. "Tell me you didn't."

"I didn't do anything." At least nothing that was Jade's business, nothing that was anybody's business, except hers and Tuck's. And they were forgetting all about it.

"You *slept* with him?"

Amber didn't want to lie, so she didn't answer.

Jade reached for her hands. "Oh, Amber. You're usually so smart."

"It wasn't stupid."

"I don't want you to get hurt."

"I'm not getting hurt. It just...happened." Amber realized how trite that sounded. "It was only the once."

"He's your boss."

"Only for a little while. Dixon will come back and then it'll all be over. Tuck barely shows up at the office."

When Dixon got back, Amber fully expected Tuck to return to his previous life. He might want to impress his father, but he wasn't likely to give up the parties and vacations in order to work his butt off.

Last night she'd had a few moments of optimism. But she knew Jackson was right. Tuck liked his life exactly the way it was. Last night Tuck had told her what he thought she wanted to hear. He probably always told women what he thought they wanted to hear.

She lowered herself onto the bedside chair. "I don't know what I was thinking."

"You were thinking he was a superhot guy. At least, that's what I'm usually thinking."

Amber gave a helpless laugh. "He was. He is. Oh, man, he was good."

For the first time since it happened, she let the full bloom of their lovemaking rush through her mind. It had been amazing. And she wanted to do it again, so badly.

"At least there's that," Jade said softly.

"You say it as if it's a good thing."

"It's not?"

Amber straightened in the chair. "No, it's not. It would have been better to be disappointed."

"So you didn't want to do it again," Jade said with sage understanding.

"What is *wrong* with me? I'm no better than Margaret."

"Who's Margaret?"

"Tuck's father's secretary. Turns out she's having an affair with him."

"He's married?"

"Yes."

"Tuck's not married," said Jade.

"He's still my boss."

"True. But that makes it risky, not immoral. Those are two totally different circumstances."

"It was a mistake," Amber said, more to herself than to Jade. "But I'm over it. I can do that. I'm tough." She drew a bracing breath. "Now, what about you? Is everything still looking good?"

Jade's hand moved to her stomach. "She's kicking less. I bet it must be getting crowded in there."

"Is that normal?" Amber's gaze rested on Jade's bulging stomach.

"The doc says it often happens that way. My back is absolutely killing me." Jade moved and stretched in the bed.

"I'm sorry."

"And I've got heartburn and an overactive bladder. I'll be so glad when this is over."

"It won't be much longer," said Amber, feeling sympathetic. "I've been thinking I better get shopping. Have you thought about what you'll need? Can you make me a list?"

"You don't have to buy me things."

"You're going to need a crib and diapers."

"There's a secondhand store on Grand. We could check there after I get home."

"Sure," said Amber, knowing the least she could do was to buy her new niece a crib. She didn't want to make Jade feel bad about her financial circumstances, so she'd figure out the necessities on her own and get them ready.

"I should head for the office," she said, coming to her feet.

She wasn't looking forward to it, but she was confident that the more time she spent around Tuck in the office, the easier it would be to keep her feelings in perspective.

"In a way, it's reassuring," said Jade, a look of contentment on her face.

"What is?"

"To know you're not perfect."

"Who ever said I was perfect?"

"Mom, me, you."

"Me?" Amber couldn't imagine when or why she would have said that.

"You don't remember the straight As?"

"I didn't get straight As."

"You got a B plus in tenth-grade math."

"See?"

Amber remembered it well. It was a blight on the report card, as if someone had painted a black, hairy spider in the middle of a butterfly collage.

"You set your alarm for six fifty-three every morning."

It had made perfect sense to Amber. "I liked to lay there for two minutes before getting out of bed."

"You knew all the food groups. You talked about them at every meal."

"We didn't always have them."

"We never had them. But you knew what they were. I remember Mom giving us each five dollars for candy. She was drunk, of course, in an 'I love you, kids' mood."

Amber didn't like to remember her sloppy, tearful mother professing her love for them. It was inevitably followed by a monologue of self-pity, then a rant about how they didn't love her back. Then she'd vomit and pass out in the bathroom. More often than not, leaving a mess for Amber to clean up.

"Don't go back there," she said softly to Jade.

"I spent it all on chocolate," said Jade. "You bought chewable vitamins. I was baffled."

"I don't remember that," said Amber, searching her memory for the incident.

"You were perfect," said Jade.

"You make me sound pretentious and superior." What could Amber have been trying to prove?

"You didn't want us to die of scurvy."

But they hadn't been on the verge of malnutrition.

"We had juice with breakfast most mornings," said Amber.

"I hate to admit it, but part of me is glad you jumped into bed with your boss. If you're not all good, then maybe I'm not all bad."

"You're not bad, Jade."

"I'm pretty bad."

"No. And anyway, you're getting better."

"I'm trying."

"I'll try, too," said Amber.

"Try to do what? Be worse?"

"Be, I don't know... Normal, I guess, less uptight and judgmental. Those are not attractive qualities."

Jade grimaced as she shifted her back to a new position. "I realize now that you were trying to hold chaos together with your bare hands."

"Maybe I should have let it go."

Maybe if she had, Jade wouldn't have run away. Maybe if she hadn't been so morally superior, they could have worked together.

Then it came to her that she should do the same thing now—let things go. It was none of her business what Tuck did or didn't do with Tucker Transportation. Dixon's decisions were similarly his own. Why did she feel an obligation to control the situation?

"I can't see you doing that." Jade looked amused.

"A month ago, I wouldn't have been able to picture you writing your GED."

"Those are opposites."

"Not really."

"Don't change, Amber. I need you just the way you are."

For some reason, Amber's eyes teared up. She quickly blinked.

"I won't change," she promised. At least not so that Jade could see. But she wasn't going to badger Tuck anymore. Nobody needed that. She was surprised he'd put up with it this long.

Jamison's eyes were closed, his expression lax, and his wrinkled skin was sallow against the stark white of the hospital sheets. Machines whirred and beeped as Tuck moved cautiously toward the bedside, screens glowing and colored dots of LED lights blinking in different rhythms. There was an oxygen tube beneath Jamison's nose and an IV line in his arm.

It was odd seeing him like this. Tuck half expected him to open his eyes, sit up and bellow out orders.

"Dad?" Tuck said softly.

Sounds from the hallway drifted through the glass door and windows: a phone ringing, a nurse's voice, a cart wheeling by and the ping of an elevator.

"Dad?" he repeated.

Jamison's pale blue eyes fluttered open, looking cloudy instead of sharp.

"Hi, Dad," said Tuck.

He felt as though he ought to squeeze his father's hand or stroke his brow. But they didn't have that kind of relationship. There was no tenderness between them. Wary suspicion interspersed with crisp cordiality was more their style.

"Dixon?" Jamison rasped, then he coughed and grimaced with the effort.

"It's Tuck," said Tuck.

Jamison squinted. "Where's Dixon?"

"He's still away."

"Away where?"

"Sailing," said Tuck.

"On the lake?"

"Off the coast of California." Tuck paused. "I've been taking care of things while he's gone."

Jamison's frown deepened. Then he waved a dismissive hand, the IV tube clattering against the bed rail. "Where's your mother?"

Tuck pulled in a chair and sat down. "She's with Aunt Julie."

"Why?"

"Dad, you know you're in Boston, right?"

Jamison looked confused for a moment, then his brow furrowed deeply and he looked annoyed. "Yes, I know I'm in Boston."

"And you understand that you had a heart attack." Tuck was growing concerned with his father's apparent level of confusion.

"You must be feeling pleased with yourself." Jamison's voice seemed stronger. He gripped on to the bed rails.

"How so?"

"You got rid of me. And you've sent Dixon off somewhere. What have you been up to without us?"

Ah, yes. Tuck's father was back.

"I didn't give you a heart attack, Dad."

"I want to see your brother."

"Get in line," said Tuck. Then he regretted the sarcasm. "Dixon can't be reached right now."

"Of course he can. Call him."

"He's out of cell range."

"Then, send somebody after him, write a letter, use a carrier pigeon for all I care."

Tuck spoke slowly and clearly. "Dixon is gone. I can't find him and I can't get him back. That's why I'm here."

"This is nonsense," Jamison growled. "Just because I'm here in this hospital bed doesn't mean you can lie to me."

"I'm not lying to you."

"The business can't run without Dixon."

"It is running without Dixon, Dad. It's been running without Dixon for nearly two months."

Jamison opened his mouth, but Tuck kept on talking. "I'm here for your proxy."

Jamison's eyes bugged out. "My *what*?"

"I've held off as long as I can. But I need to make some decisions. I need to hire new executives and I need a proxy vote for your shares."

"It'll be a cold day in hell before I give you control of Tucker Transportation."

"It's only temporary."

"Where's Dixon?"

Tuck leaned slightly forward. "Dixon's gone. He left on his own and he hasn't come back."

"What's going on? Why are you doing this?" Jamison groped for the nurse call button and pressed it.

Tuck pushed back the chair and came to his feet. "I'm not *doing* anything. I'm jumping in to run your precious company."

"You don't know how to run the company."

"You're right about that."

The two men stared at each other.

A nurse breezed into the room.

"Mr. Tucker?" she asked. "Is something wrong?"

"Yes, something is wrong," Jamison stormed. "My son is telling me lies."

The nurse looked to Tuck and he gave a slight shake of his head.

"Are you in any pain?" The nurse checked his IV.

"I'm not in pain. My other son, Dixon, can you bring him here? I need to talk to him."

"I'm going to check your blood pressure." As she spoke, the nurse wrapped Jamison's arm in a blood-pressure cuff.

"Dad," Tuck began again, "you're in no condition to attend a board meeting."

Jamison tried to sit up.

"Oh, no, you don't," said the nurse, placing a hand on his shoulder. Her tone was calm but firm. "Your blood pressure is slightly elevated."

"Is that dangerous?" asked Tuck, wondering if he should leave.

"Only slightly," said the nurse. She frowned at Jamison. "You try to stay calm."

"I'm perfectly calm."

The nurse moved to the foot of the bed, making notes on the chart.

"Harvey Miller resigned," Tuck told his father.

"We have no finance director?"

"No."

"What did you do?"

"Nothing. He moved to a different company. People do that sometimes."

"Where did he go?"

"That's irrelevant. The important point is that I need to replace him. To do that, I need to formalize my position as interim president. So I need your proxy to vote your shares."

"You can't be president."

"Okay," said Tuck, thoroughly tired of this argument and every other one he'd had for the past decade. "I won't be president." He turned to leave.

"Dixon can be interim president."

"Sounds good," Tuck called over his shoulder. "Let me know how it all turns out."

"Bring him here," Jamison shouted out.

"Calm down," said the nurse.

Tuck stopped and turned back. "I'm sure he'll show up eventually. Until then, well, Tucker Transportation will have to survive without a finance director and without a president. I'm sure it'll be fine. After all, anything's better than having me in charge, isn't it?"

"Insolent," said Jamison.

"So you always say. I'm here. I'm offering to help. Take it or leave it. It's entirely up to you."

Jamison glared at him while the machines beeped his vital signs, the hospital hallway buzzed with activity and the nurse refilled his plastic water jug. Tuck almost felt sorry for his father—almost. Even when the man was all but desperate for Tuck's assistance, he'd only grudgingly accept it. How was that supposed to make a person feel?

"I'll give you my proxy," said Jamison. "Time limited."

"Fine," said Tuck.

He reached into his inside jacket pocket as he returned to the bed, producing the letter his lawyer had crafted. "We can both initial on an end date."

He approached the bed and maneuvered his father's tray into position. Then he jotted down a date one month away and stroked his initials next to the addition.

"I need my glasses," Jamison muttered.

Tuck spotted the glasses on the bedside table and handed them to his father. Then he handed over the pen and watched while Jamison signed over formal control of the company. Butterflies rose up unexpectedly in his stomach.

He didn't want this. He'd never sought it out. But now that he had it, he found he didn't want to fail.

Ten

"This was all your doing," Tuck said to Amber as he gazed at the aftermath of the party in the huge, high-ceilinged living room of his family's home.

Though staff had been ubiquitous throughout, she could see the mansion showed the effects of hosting two hundred people. The midnight buffet was being cleared away by the catering staff and the few glasses left on side tables were being dispatched to the kitchen.

"It doesn't look that bad," she responded.

He pulled at the end of his bow tie, releasing the knot. "I'm not blaming you for the mess."

"Then, what?"

He gestured to an armchair next to the marble fireplace.

Grateful, she sank down on the soft cream-colored leather. It was a relief to get off the four-inch heels.

Tuck sat in the opposite chair. "You convinced me I could do it."

"Throw a party?"

Tuck was nothing if not a party guy. She had to assume he'd thrown dozens, if not hundreds, of parties himself over the years.

"I meant run the company. If you hadn't pushed me to start making decisions, I never would have gone to see my father."

"And if you hadn't gone to see your father."

"I wouldn't have hired Samuel and Gena."

"I like Samuel and Gena."

"So do I. I'm not sure how my father's going to feel about them."

"Because they're too young to have such responsible jobs?" The two were both in their early thirties.

"I'm sure they won't fit his image of an executive."

"Do you think clients will care that Samuel wears blue jeans?" asked Amber.

"Lucas wears blue jeans."

"Operations and marketing are two different functions."

"True," Tuck agreed. "Thirsty? You want some ice water?"

"Sure."

Amber expected him to rise and pour some water at the bar. Instead, he subtly raised a hand and a staff member was instantly by his side.

"Yes, sir?" said the neatly dressed waiter.

"Can you bring us some ice water?"

"Right away, sir." The man withdrew.

Amber could only stare at Tuck for a moment.

"What?" he asked.

"Even knowing you were so rich, I didn't picture all this."

He gazed around at the soaring ceilings, wooden pillars and expensive oil paintings. "It is rather ostentatious."

"Flick of a finger and the ice water appears."

"I thought you were thirsty."

"I thought we'd pour it ourselves."

"Aah. You're uncomfortable with the household staff."

"I'm baffled by the notion of household staff."

"It's a big house," said Tuck.

"That doesn't mean you can't pour your own water."

"Are you calling me spoiled?"

"I always call you spoiled."

To her surprise, he shrugged. "Fair criticism. If it helps, I often pour my own water, and my own whiskey. I even go so far as to open my own beer bottle."

She couldn't help but grin. "Then, I take it all back. You're obviously a self-sufficient man."

The waiter returned, setting down a silver tray with two glasses and a pitcher.

"Shall I pour, sir?" he asked.

"We'll be fine, thanks," Tuck answered with a wry grin.

The man left.

"Okay, now you're just trying to impress me," said Amber.

Tuck sat up and leaned forward. "Is it working?" He poured them each a glass, handing one to her.

"Be still, my beating heart."

"You do know it's not always like this."

"Always like what?"

"This many staff members, hanging out in the living room, dressed in a tux." He tugged off the tie and undid his top button. "Other parts of the house are a lot less formal."

She found herself glancing around again. "I would hope so. I'd be jumpy if I had to live in this 24/7."

He took a sip of his water. "Want to know a secret?"

"Has anyone ever said no to that question?"

He chuckled. "I guess not."

"Then, yes, do tell me your secret." She took a long drink, realizing she was very thirsty after a martini and two glasses of wine.

"The place makes me jumpy, too."

"Yeah, right." She continued drinking the water.

"I never liked this room. Or the library. You should see the library. Talk about pretentious and forbidding. My dad's fortress. It's positively gothic." He lowered his tone. "Nothing good ever happens in the library."

"Now you really have got me curious."

"You sure you're brave enough to see the library?"

"Oh, I'm brave enough. Besides, your father's not here."

"Check out the lion's den while the lion's away." He set down his glass. "You're very smart. That's what I like about you."

She gave a saucy grin at the compliment, but it also warmed her heart. It was nice to think that Tuck considered her intelligent. She'd certainly gained great respect for his reasoning and judgment. She'd also come to respect his hard work.

The past two weeks, she'd found herself wondering if he'd always been industrious, but simply focused on things other than Tucker Transportation. There was no doubt he'd raised the bar on being Chicago's preeminent playboy bachelor.

He came to his feet. "Let's go."

She rose and grimaced as her shoes pinched down on her swollen feet.

"Something wrong?" he asked.

"Would it be terribly rude if I took off my shoes?"

His mouth broke into a mischievous smile. "Shoeless in the library. You're a maverick, Amber, no doubt about it."

"Good thing your father's not around to see this." She peeled off the shoes and dropped them to the carpet.

"I may send him a picture."

"And get me fired?"

Tuck headed across the room and she fell into step beside him.

"Nobody's going to fire you," he said.

"You did."

"I was mistaken. And I've learned my lesson."

"Jamison was about to fire me. Dixon's the only one who hasn't wanted to send me packing."

"What do you mean Jamison was about to fire you?"

"When he had his heart attack," she admitted. "When I wouldn't tell him anything about Dixon. I swear the next words out of his mouth would have been *you're fired*."

"But he had a heart attack instead."

"I wasn't glad," she hastily told him, assailed by a wave of guilt. "I mean, even to save my job, I would never wish a heart attack on anyone. Maybe I should have told somebody. I guess that would have been you. Should I have told you? Or… Oh, no, do you think it was my fault?"

"Wow." Tuck came to a stop in the hallway, canting his body to face her. "You just did a whole big thing there all by yourself."

He seemed unusually tall, unusually imposing and unusually impressive.

"I really hadn't given it enough thought before," she said. "The man had a heart attack because I refused to help him. I'm not sure I deserve to keep my job."

"My father had a heart attack because of one too many rib eyes, and a fondness for chocolate truffles and Cuban cigars. Don't beat yourself up." Tuck put his hand on the knob of a dark paneled door. "Are you ready?"

"I'm not sure I'm through feeling guilty."

"Yes, you are. Of all the stressors in his life, you'd be ranked near the bottom. If you want to blame anyone, blame Dixon."

"Dixon *had* to get away."

"Yeah, yeah. We all know your opinion on that. Then, blame me. Or maybe blame Margaret. Keeping his affair a secret had to be stressful."

Amber couldn't argue with that. Tuck pushed the door and it yawned open.

As she walked in, antique lamps came up around the perimeter of the rectangular room, giving it a yellowish glow. The ceilings were arched, the woodwork dark and intricately carved and the books were lined on recessed shelves, secured behind fronts of black metal latticework.

There were clusters of armchairs with worn leather upholstery. And in the center of the room was an oblong table, set on two massive pedestals and surrounded by eight antique chairs, upholstered in burgundy damask.

"I can picture him here," she said, her voice sounding small in the imposing space.

"I try not to," said Tuck. Then he unexpectedly took her hand. "Come here."

"Why?" A flutter of reaction made its way up her arm, crossing into her chest. She was instantly aware of Tuck as a man, her attraction to him and the fact that they were completely alone.

"I want you to sit."

"Why?"

"Here." He pointed to one of the armchairs.

"What are you doing?" She didn't know what he had planned, but something in his voice was arousing her.

"Sit," he said softly.

She did.

"I want to picture you there," said Tuck. "With no shoes." He unexpectedly reached around her and unclasped her hair, letting it fall around her face. "Perfect," he said.

Then he paused, his gaze squinting down.

"What?" She felt suddenly self-conscious.

"One more thing." He reached out again, sliding his index finger under the spaghetti strap of her silver-and-ice-blue cocktail dress, dropping it down off her shoulder.

Her arousal ramped up, sending pleasure impulses along her thighs. She gazed up at him, unable to speak.

He took a step back. "*That's* what I'm going to remember in this room."

Her entire body heated under his gaze.

He watched her intently for a full minute, his eyes dark and clouded with obvious desire.

"You want to see my favorite room?" he asked.

She knew she should say no. It was the only reasonable answer. His question could mean anything and everything.

But her lips stubbornly formed the word *yes*.

Amber looked surprised when they entered the second-floor sitting room. Tuck could only imagine that she'd expected something bigger and grander. She gazed at the earthy rattan furniture, the watercolors on the walls and the stoneware vases atop pale maple tables.

"Not what you were expecting?" he asked.

"Not even close." She ran her hand over the back of the sofa, moving farther into the room.

With her bare feet, loose hair and the spaghetti strap still drooping over her shoulder, she seemed to belong here. She'd looked great in the library, the juxtaposition of such a feminine woman in such a masculine room. But here she looked fantastic. He wanted to close the door, lock out the world and maybe keep her here forever.

"It keeps me grounded," he told her.

"I've never thought of you as being grounded." Her pretty smile took some of the sting out of the words.

"What do you think of me as being?"

"Indulged, cosseted, lucky."

"I suppose I'm all of those things." He saw no point in denying it.

"It's more complicated than that." She looped around and came back to him.

"Nice of you to say so."

"I'm only being honest."

"Then, nice of you to notice," he said.

"It took me a while to notice." She stopped in front of him, all fresh faced and adorable. Her skin was satin smooth above the dress, lips a perfect pink, her hair just mussed enough to be off-the-charts sexy.

He remembered her naked. He remembered every single nuance of her body, the curve of her hip, the swell of her breasts, the blue of her eyes as passion overwhelmed her.

"Took me about half a second to notice you," he said gruffly.

"What did you notice?" She was so close, it was about to drive him crazy.

The slightest movement of his hand and he'd be touching her waist, feeling the pulse of her skin. If he leaned in, just a few inches, he could kiss her. Or at least find out if she'd let him kiss her. He picked up the scent of her hair. His fingertips twitched with the memory of her skin.

"Your eyes," he said. "Your shoes and your sassy mouth."

"Somebody has to keep you in line."

He eased slightly closer. "You want to keep me in line?"

She didn't answer, but her eyes darkened to indigo.

"Know what I want to do to you?" he asked softly.

Her lips parted.

He moved closer still, twining one hand with hers. He brushed back her hair, leaned in close to her ear.

"Kiss you," he whispered. "Pull you into my arms. Peel that dress from your body and make long, slow love to you."

"That wasn't..." Her voice went breathless. "What I was expecting."

"No?" He placed a kiss on her shoulder, reveling in the sweetness of her skin.

"I'm lying."

He kissed her again, closer to the crook of her neck. "Yeah?"

"It was exactly what I was expecting."

"But you came up here with me anyway?" His lips brushed her skin as he spoke.

"Yes." Her palms touched his chest, warm and intimate. "I want you, Tuck. I keep trying to ignore it."

He drew back to look into her eyes. "I can't ignore it."

"I feel as if we need to..." She toyed with a button on his dress shirt.

"Make love?"

"Set some ground rules."

He tenderly kissed her lips. "Sure. Whatever you want."

"This can't impact our working relationship."

He cradled her chin with his palm, kissing her again. He didn't see how that was possible, but he wasn't about to disagree. "Okay."

"You can't fire me, or promote me, or give me any better or worse treatment because I'm..."

"Completely and totally blowing my mind?"

"Tuck."

"I'm not going to fire you."

"Or promote me."

"Maybe. Probably. I think I pretty much already have. You want a new title?"

"You're not listening."

He kissed her again. "You're very distracting."

She pressed against him, her body molding to his. "We have to get this straight."

"Keep the boardroom out of the bedroom." He wrapped his arms around her, sighing in complete contentment. Up against him, wrapped around him, that was where she belonged. That was where he wanted her to stay.

"Right." She sounded surprised.

"Then, shut up, Amber. We're a long way from the boardroom."

He kissed her and passion roared to life within him.

She kissed him back, coming up on her toes, her arms winding around his neck. He tipped his head to deepen the kiss, pressing the small of her back, arching her body, inserting his thigh between her bare legs.

She groaned his name. Then she went for his belt, his button, his fly, her small hand all but searing him with need.

"Amber, don't." He could feel his control slip away.

"I can't wait," she rasped. "I've waited, and I'm done waiting."

She didn't have to wait.

He reached beneath her dress and stripped off her panties. Then he dropped into a chair, sitting her straight and square in his lap. She loosened his slacks and eased herself down. She was hot and tight, and each inch was a straight shot to paradise.

He bracketed her hips and pushed himself home.

She braced her hands on his shoulders. Her head tipped back. "Oh, yes," she whispered.

"You're amazing," he told her. "Fantastic. Spectacular."

Her nails dug in and her thighs tightened around him. He lost track of time as their pace increased. His world contracted and then disappeared. There was nothing but Amber. He didn't end and she didn't begin. They were fused to one and he needed to hold on to that forever.

She cried out his name and the sound pierced straight through him. Her body contracted and pulsed, and he followed her over the edge in a cascade of heat and sensation. He dropped back on the chair, cradled her face with his hands, pulled her down for a kiss, tasting her, breathing her, feeling life pulse through her, willing the euphoria to last forever.

Then he cradled her close, thinking how perfectly she fit against him.

"Stay," he murmured in her ear. "I want you in my bed. I want you in my arms. The night in Arizona was sheer torture after you left me."

Her chest rose and fell against his, the sound of her deep breaths echoing through the silent room.

"Okay," she finally said.

He drew back. "Okay?"

She nodded.

"Okay," he said, his body relaxing with relief. "Okay."

Amber's ringtone woke her from a sound sleep. She was instantly aware of Tuck's naked body wrapped around her, the faint sandalwood scent of his sheets and the sound of a fan whirring above the big bed. The phone rang again.

She pushed up on her elbow and groped for the bedside table. Tuck groaned and moved beside her. A moment later, the room was flooded with light. Her phone rang a third time as she blinked to adjust her eyes.

"Did you find it?" he asked.

"Yes. It's here." She fumbled with her cell as she answered, clumsy with sleep. "Hello?"

"Amber Bowen?" The woman's voice was crisp.

"Yes. It's me."

"This is Brandy Perkins calling. I'm a nurse at Memorial Hospital."

Amber sat straight up. "Hi, Yes." She had met Brandy a number of times. "Is something wrong?"

"Can you come into Maternity right away?"

"Yes, of course." Amber swung her legs to the side of the bed. "Is Jade all right?"

Tuck sat up beside her.

"Her blood pressure has taken an unexpected spike."

Tuck's hand cradled her bare shoulder, his voice deep and soft. "Something wrong?"

"The baby has gone into distress, and we're performing an emergency C-section."

"I'm on my way." Amber rose from the bed as she ended the call.

Tuck's voice was sharper, more alert. "What's wrong?"

"I need to get to the hospital. It's Jade." Amber tracked down her panties, stepping into them and locating her bra.

He rocked to his feet. "I'll drive you."

"No. That's okay. I've got my car."

"You're upset. You shouldn't drive yourself." He was dressing as he spoke.

"I don't know how long I'll be."

"So what?"

"So I want to take my car."

Her dress on, she headed for the bedroom door. Her shoes were still down in the library. She was pretty sure she remembered the way back.

Tuck followed. "What happened?"

"It's her blood pressure. The baby's in distress and they have to do an emergency Caesarean. I knew there was a chance, but things were looking so good. I didn't expect..."

She knew Jade's condition could be life threatening, for both Jade and the baby. But she hadn't wanted to face that possibility. She'd been too optimistic, too cavalier about the potential danger.

She should have paid more attention to how Jade was feeling. Maybe if she'd spent more time at the hospital instead of throwing a party and sleeping with Tuck. What if she'd left her phone in her purse downstairs and didn't hear it ring? What if the battery had died overnight?

"Jade's already at the hospital?" Tuck asked as they took the stairs.

"She's been there for two weeks."

"Why didn't you say something?"

"Say what?"

Amber's personal life was another thing she was keeping separate. Tuck had barely even met Jade.

"Tell me something that big was going on in your life."

"Why?" She entered the library.

Luckily, the lights were still on, and she quickly located her shoes.

"Oh, I don't know," said Tuck. "Because we see each other every day."

"Only because we work together."

She marched toward the living room. Her car keys were in her purse. She was maybe thirty minutes from the hospital, twenty-five if traffic was light, which it ought to be at 3:00 a.m.

"Right," said Tuck, a strange tone in his voice. "We work together. That's all."

She paused to take in his expression. "I have to go to my sister right now."

"I'll drive you."

"No, you won't. Good night, Tuck."

"It's morning."

She didn't even know how to respond to that. She left through the front door, taking the long driveway past the brick entry pillars and onto the street.

Traffic was blessedly light and she was able to find a good parking spot at the hospital. She rushed through the lobby, going directly to Jade's room. She knew her sister wouldn't be there, but she hoped the nurses could give her some information.

Brandy was at the nurse's station.

"How is she?" Amber asked, realizing she was winded.

"Still in surgery," said Brandy.

Amber didn't like the look on the woman's face. All the way here, she'd been telling herself it was going to be fine. Jade was going to be fine. The baby was going to be fine.

Amber swallowed. "How bad?"

Brandy came around the end of the counter. "She had a seizure."

Amber felt her knees go weak.

Brandy took her arm. "Let's sit down."

"Is she..." Amber couldn't bring herself to ask the question. "What about the baby?"

"They're doing everything they can." Brandy led her toward a sitting area in a small alcove.

"I don't like the sound of that." It was not at all reassuring.

Brandy sat next to her on a narrow vinyl sofa. "The baby is very close to term."

"So she has a fighting chance."

"Very much so," said Brandy.

"And all I can do is wait."

"I know it's hard."

Amber nodded. She was sitting here wondering if her sister and her niece were going to live or die.

"Can I get you something?" asked Brandy. "There's coffee in the corner or water?"

"I'm fine."

"Would you like to freshen up?"

Amber glanced down at her dress and realized how she must look. She hadn't removed her makeup before tumbling into bed with Tuck. It was probably smeared under her eyes. Her hair had to be a fright.

"That bad?" she asked the nurse.

Brandy gave her a smile. "You'll be able to see Jade once she wakes up, not to mention hold the baby. You don't want to scare them."

"Yes," said Amber. "Let's think positively."

A woman in scrubs came through a set of double doors.

Brandy took Amber's hand and Amber's heart sank through the floor.

They rose together.

"Dr. Foster, this is Jade's sister, Amber," said Brandy.

"Jade is weak," the doctor said without preamble. "We had to restart her heart."

Amber's legs nearly gave way.

"She's in recovery," said Dr. Foster. "Her vital signs have stabilized and her blood pressure is under control."

"She'll be all right?" Amber felt the need to confirm.

"We expect her to make a full recovery."

"And the baby?"

The doctor smiled. "The baby is healthy. A girl."

"I have a niece?"

"She's in the nursery. You can see her if you want."

Amber gave a rapid nod, her eyes tearing up. Worry rose up from her shoulders and she felt instantly light.

Eleven

As soon as Amber had left the mansion, Tuck realized he'd been a total jerk. Her sister was having emergency surgery. What did it matter if he and Amber's relationship was up in the air? They could talk about it tomorrow, or the day after that, or the day after that.

She'd made love with him. Then she'd spent the night with him. He'd reveled in holding her naked in his arms, joking and laughing with her. He'd looked forward to breakfast together, mentally filing away another image of her in his family home.

Instead, he'd showered and changed, stopped to pick her up some coffee and a bagel and made his way to the hospital. She had to be exhausted, and distressed, and he was determined to make up for his behavior. She needed his support right now. She didn't need him arguing with her.

It took some time to locate the maternity wing. But once there, he was told visiting hours didn't start until seven and he had to wait in the lobby. He gave in and drank both cups of lukewarm coffee, finally getting on the elevator with the blueberry bagels for Amber.

As he approached the room, he could hear her voice. It was melodic and soothing.

"She's incredible," she was saying.

"Isn't she?" Jade responded, her voice sounding slightly weak.

Tuck paused to brace his hand on the wall, relief rushing through him. He hadn't realized he'd been that worried.

"Thank you," said Jade. "For being here. For helping us."

"Don't be silly," Amber responded. "Of course I'm here, and of course I'm helping."

"You always do."

"She has your eyes," said Amber.

"I thought of a name."

"You did?"

"After you. I'm going to name her Amber."

For some reason, Tuck's chest went tight.

"I don't know," said Amber.

"We owe you so much."

"I'm her aunt. It's my job, and she doesn't owe me a thing. Look at that face, those blue eyes, that tiny nose."

There was a silent pause.

"I think," Amber continued, "that she's her very own little person. She deserves her very own name."

"You think?" asked Jade.

"I'm sure. Thank you. Really, it's a wonderful thought."

There was a pause and Tuck took a step forward.

"What about Crystal?" asked Jade.

"Another rock?" There was a trace of laughter in Amber's voice.

"You're solid as a rock," said Jade.

"So are you," said Amber.

"And she will be, too."

"Crystal. I love it. It's perfect."

Tuck knew he should either walk away or announce himself, but something kept him still and silent.

"Do you think the three of us can become a family?" asked Jade, a catch in her voice. "The way we never were."

"Yes," Amber said softly. "You, me and Crystal. We can do that."

"No creepy boyfriends."

Tuck found he didn't like the sound of that. He wasn't creepy. Then again, he wasn't a boyfriend.

"No unreliable men," Amber stated firmly.

Did she think of him as unreliable? She probably did. She probably thought Dixon was more reliable, which wasn't fair, given the current circumstances.

He gave himself a mental head slap. If he didn't want to keep hearing things he didn't like, he needed to stop eavesdropping.

"She's never going to be frightened," said Jade, as Tuck moved for the door. "Or hungry, or lonely."

"We'll keep her safe."

"I'll get a job," said Jade.

"Not today, you won't."

He knocked softly on the open door. "Hello."

Amber looked up. She was sitting in a chair at the bedside covered in a pale green hospital gown, a pink bundle in her arms. He couldn't see the baby's face, but she had a head of dark hair—a brunette like her aunt.

Jade was propped up in the bed, looking exhausted, her face pale, her hair flattened against her head.

"Tuck." Amber was obviously surprised to see him.

"I wanted to make sure everything was okay." He glanced at the paper bag in his hands, realizing he should have brought flowers or maybe a teddy bear.

"Hi, Tuck," said Jade. She seemed less surprised and gave him a tired smile.

"Congratulations, Jade." He moved to get a better view of the baby. "She's beautiful."

"Isn't she?" asked Jade.

"Are you okay?" he asked, giving in to an urge to squeeze her hand.

"Sore. But I'm going to be fine."

"I'm very glad to hear that."

His attention went back to Amber and the baby. She looked good with a baby in her arms, natural, radiant.

"How did you know I was here?" asked Jade.

Amber's eyes widened.

Tuck paused to see how she'd answer.

She didn't.

"Were you with him last night?" asked Jade.

She was very quick on the uptake for someone who'd just had surgery.

"It was a corporate party," said Tuck.

"We spent the night together," said Amber.

Her answer thrilled him. Yes, they'd spent the night together. And he didn't care who knew it.

"Sorry to interrupt," said Jade, glancing between them.

Tuck grinned with amazement. "You had to have one of the best excuses ever."

Jade chuckled and then groaned with obvious pain.

"I'm sorry," he quickly told her.

"Don't apologize for being funny."

"I didn't mean for it to hurt."

Crystal let out a little cry.

"It does," said Jade. "I hate to whine, but it hurts a lot."

"Do you need me to get the nurse?" he asked.

Crystal wiggled in Amber's arms, emitting a few more subdued cries.

"Maybe you should," said Jade, holding out her arms to take Crystal. "I want to try to feed her again. You should go home," she said to Amber.

"No way."

"Get some rest. Take a shower."

"I don't need to rest."

"Yes, you do."

Amber hesitated.

"I can drop you," said Tuck.

"I have my car." She stood to hand the baby to Jade. "Okay, but I'm coming back."

"I would hope so."

Tuck started for the corridor to find a nurse.

Amber's voice followed him. "Goodbye, sweetheart."

He knew she was talking to the baby, but he loved the word anyway.

He located a nurse and then met Amber in the hallway.

"You look exhausted."

"I am *so* relieved." She pulled off the gown, revealing last night's dress. "Her heart actually stopped."

Tuck automatically reached for Amber, pulling her to him. "How can I help?"

"I'm fine. I was terrified, but I'm fine now."

"Let me take you home."

"There's no need."

"It'll make me feel better. I need to do something useful."

"You're very useful. You signed up four new accounts last night."

"I mean useful to you."

"You're keeping the company afloat, keeping me in a job, helping me pay my bills."

Tuck drew back, a bolt of comprehension lighting up his brain. "Twenty-eight thousand, two hundred and sixty-three dollars."

"Huh?"

"Jade was already in the hospital when you came back. That was the amount on her bill. You asked for a signing bonus. You agreed to help me. You did it all because of her."

He could tell by Amber's expression that he'd hit the nail on the head. Then he wondered what else she'd done because of her sister.

He backed off. "Is that why you're helping me with the company?"

"In part, yes. I need a job right now, Tuck. More than I've ever needed a job in my life."

He loosened his hold on her and drew back. "And the rest?"

Her expression narrowed. "The rest is the rest." She didn't elaborate and he didn't jump in. "I hope you're not asking if I slept with you to protect my job and support my sister."

He was. No, he wasn't. He wasn't, but he couldn't help but worry that her behavior with him was laced with complexities.

"Don't worry about it," she said.

"Don't worry about *what*?"

"I'm going home to change." She glanced down at her dress. "I look ridiculous. I'll see you at the office tomorrow."

She tossed the hospital gown in a nearby bin and turned for the elevators.

He wanted to call her back. He needed to understand where she was coming from, what she was feeling for him, what last night had meant to her. But he couldn't let himself be selfish again. She'd had a rough night. Jade needed her. And Tuck was simply going to have to wait to find out where he stood among everything else in Amber's life.

They might have spent the night together…well, half the night together. But everything Amber knew about Tuck remained true. No matter how tempting it was to let him drive her home and comfort her, she couldn't let herself pretend they were in a relationship. He was her boss, not her boyfriend. At best, they were having a fling. At worst, she was a two-night stand.

She had Jade and she had her new niece, Crystal. They were her family, her personal life, her emotional support. It wasn't Tuck.

In the office Monday morning, she steeled herself to see him. She dropped her purse into her desk drawer and plunked down on her chair. She told herself they'd worked the party together like a practiced team, picking up on each other's cues, making clients laugh and agree and, most important, closing the deal.

That had to be enough. It was *going* to be enough. She scrunched her eyes shut and gritted her teeth. She wasn't going to allow herself to want more.

"Good morning, Amber." Dixon's voice nearly startled her out of her chair.

"Dixon?" she squeaked, her eyes popping open.

He looked tanned and toned and totally relaxed.

"I'm back," he said simply.

"Where? How?"

Dixon wasn't the hugging type, so she didn't jump up to embrace him.

His smile faded. "I heard about my dad. I flew straight to Boston yesterday and then I came here."

"Welcome back." She was happy to see him.

She told herself it was an enormous relief to have him here. Things could get back to normal now. She could stop juggling so many problems and Tuck—

She swallowed. Tuck could get back to normal, too.

"He in there?" Dixon cocked his head to Tuck's closed office door.

"I think so."

"Great." Dixon's intelligent gaze took in the clutter on her desk. "Looks as if you're busy."

"It's been busy," she agreed.

"But you'll move back to my office?"

"Of course I will. Right away."

"Good."

"How was your trip?"

"Enlightening."

"You feel better? You look better."

"I feel better than ever. I can't wait to get back to it."

"Great. That's great."

Tucker Transportation would be in experienced hands once again.

Just then, Tuck's office door opened. He appeared in the doorway and instantly spotted Dixon.

From behind her desk, Amber could feel Tuck's shock. His expression seemed to register disappointment. But then it quickly went to neutral.

"Dixon." Tuck's tone was neutral, too.

"Tuck," Dixon answered evenly.

"You're back."

"You're about the twenty-fifth person to say that."

Tuck glanced at Amber.

"I said it, too," she said into what felt like an awkward silence.

"You know about Dad?" Tuck asked.

Neither man moved toward the other, and she was struck by the wariness of their attitudes. Dixon had to be wondering if Tuck was angry. She couldn't tell what Tuck was thinking.

"I saw him yesterday," said Dixon.

"But you didn't call? Didn't think to give me a heads-up?"

It was Dixon's turn to glance at Amber and then at Tuck. "Should we step inside your office?"

Tuck crossed his arms over his chest. "I don't know why. You seem to like to keep Amber more informed than you keep your own brother."

Dixon seemed taken aback.

"She didn't give you away," said Tuck, finally taking a step forward.

Amber found herself glancing anxiously down the hall, worried that other staff might overhear their argument.

"I fired her," said Tuck. "And she still wouldn't tell me your secrets."

Now Dixon looked confused.

"Where you were," Tuck elaborated. "Where'd you go?"

"*Why* would you fire Amber?"

"Insubordination."

"No way."

"To me, not you."

Amber couldn't stand it any longer. "Tuck, please."

Tuck gave a cold smile. "The loyalty's returned just like that." He snapped his fingers. "I guess it never really went away."

"Amber's as loyal as they come," said Dixon.

She moved from behind her desk. "I'm going to let you two talk." She nodded at Dixon. "Maybe an office or the boardroom?"

"Good suggestion."

"She's full of them," said Tuck.

"Has he been treating you like a jerk?" Dixon's question was for Amber, but he stared at Tuck as he asked it.

Amber met Tuck's gaze. "Not at all."

Tuck stared back. "Except when I fired her."

Dixon seemed to pick up on the tension between them. "How'd you get her back?"

"Money," said Tuck.

"A signing bonus," said Amber.

Dixon grinned at that. "Well, there's no doubt she's worth it. If she'd been permanently gone, you'd be answering to me."

Tuck's jaw tightened. "As opposed to you explaining *to me* where the hell you've been for two months?"

"I suppose I owe you that."

Amber moved again, determined to leave. "You have a ten o'clock with Lucas," she told Tuck.

"Maybe," he responded.

What did that mean? Was he heading out the door before 10:00 a.m.? Now that Dixon was in the office, would Tuck simply walk out?

Good.

Great.

It really didn't matter to her either way.

With the two men sizing each other up, she quickly made her way down the hall. She'd set herself up outside Dixon's office once again. Tuck could come and say goodbye or not. It was entirely up to him.

Tuck stared at his brother across the table in the meeting room.

"I told him I needed to get away," said Dixon. "He wouldn't listen."

"I heard." Tuck didn't see any point in hiding anything. "I overheard the two of you talking in the library. I heard what he said about me as a vice president."

"Were you surprised?"

Tuck hadn't been surprised. But he had been disappointed.

"Nobody wants their father to have such a low opinion of them."

"We're talking about Jamison Tucker."

"He likes you just fine."

"Yeah," Dixon scoffed. "Well, we all know why that is."

"Because you're the anointed one."

"I mean the other."

"What other?"

Dixon stared at him in silence and obvious confusion.

"I have no idea what you're talking about," said Tuck.

"The affair."

"With Margaret?"

Dixon drew back. "Who's having an affair with Margaret?"

"Dad."

"What?" Dixon was clearly shocked. "What on earth makes you say that?"

"Because it's true. Margaret gave it away to Amber."

"It's not like Amber to gossip."

"She wasn't gossiping. Wake up, man. Do you know what you've got in Amber? The woman will practically take a bullet for you. She has more character than you can imagine."

Dixon's intelligent eyes sized him up. "Got to know her pretty well while I was gone?"

Tuck was not about to give away anything that might embarrass Amber. "Got very frustrated with her at one point." Then his mind jumped back in the conversation. "What affair were *you* talking about?"

"Mom's."

"Whoa. No way."

"You knew about it."

Tuck knew no such thing. "Who thinks Mom had an affair?"

"Dad."

"What? When? And he's living in a glass house, by the way."

"Three decades ago."

"Clearly that's relevant." Tuck knew their father's affair had gone on right up to his heart attack.

Dixon carefully enunciated his next words. "Thirty years ago. In the months *before* you were born."

Everything inside Tuck went still. "Are you saying?"

"How do you not remember that huge fight we overheard?"

"Are you saying I'm not Jamison's son?"

"You are his son. He did a DNA test years ago."

"Then, how is that the thing? Why would it make him hate me?"

"He doesn't hate you."

"He has no use for me."

"My theory," said Dixon, "is that he looks at you and remembers you could have belonged to someone else."

"That's really messed up."

Dixon scoffed out a cold laugh. "Up to now, you thought we were a normal, functional family?"

Tuck came to his feet as everything became clear. He'd never had a chance. He'd been fighting for something he couldn't possibly win. He had to get out of here, leave the company, maybe leave the city. Maybe he'd leave the state and the money behind and find his own life and career.

There was a brisk knock on the door before it opened to reveal Lucas.

Lucas didn't miss a beat when he saw Dixon. "You're back."

"I'm back."

"Good. Tuck, Gena wants to join us at ten."

"Who's Gena?" asked Dixon.

"Our new finance director."

"Why do we have a new finance director?"

"Harvey quit," said Tuck.

"Why?"

"He missed you."

"What did you do?" Dixon's tone was decidedly accusatory.

"Nothing," said Tuck, heading for the door. "Hasn't that always been the problem?"

"I'll try to get him back," said Dixon.

Tuck halted, a flash of anger hitting him. Dixon intended to reward Harvey for his disloyalty?

Tuck opened his mouth to protest, then decided not to waste his breath. Dixon was back. Tuck's father was never, *ever* going to accept him. And what Tuck liked or didn't like no longer had any relevance.

"Whatever," he said without turning. To Lucas he said, "Dixon can take the ten o'clock."

Twenty paces down the hall, he came to Amber at her old desk outside Dixon's office. She was setting out her things, settling in.

"So that's that?" he asked, struggling to come to terms with his life turning so suddenly and irrevocably upside down.

"My boss is back." She didn't pretend not to understand.

"You bailed quick enough."

"He asked me to move here."

"And what Dixon wants—"

Amber glared at Tuck.

He wanted to tell her she couldn't, that she should march back to her desk at his office to work with him, not with Dixon. He wished he had the right. He wished he had the power. Against all reason and logic, he wished his brother had never come home.

"What about you?" she asked, adjusting the angle of her computer screen.

Unlike her, he did pretend to misunderstand. "My office has been in the same place for years."

"And what are you going to do in it now?"

"Nothing."

He could take a hint. Well, maybe he couldn't take a hint. But he could understand the bald truth when it was thrown up in his face. He wasn't wanted here. And there was nothing he could do to change it. He might as well have been born to a different father.

Two months ago, it probably wouldn't have mattered. But

it mattered now. Maybe it was pride. Or maybe he liked the sense of independence and accomplishment. Or maybe he just liked Amber.

He was going to miss her.

He wasn't sure he could leave her.

"You're walking away," she said.

"I am." He had to stifle the urge to explain.

He knew she understood dysfunctional families, and he knew she'd understand what he was going through. But he couldn't presume they had a personal relationship. She'd made that clear enough at the hospital yesterday morning. She was his brother's assistant, and that was all.

"I won't be your boss anymore," he said, determined to give it one last shot.

"We both knew that would happen."

That wasn't a hint one way or the other. She wasn't giving him any help here.

"We could," he said. "You know..."

She raised her brows and looked him in the eyes.

"Date," he finally said, wondering what the heck had happened to his suave, sophisticated style.

"Each other?"

Okay, now he was just getting frustrated. "*Yes*, each other."

"Is that a good idea?"

"I'm suggesting it, aren't I?"

"You're free now, Tuck. And you're practically running for the front door. And that's fine. I understand. You never said or did a thing to suggest otherwise. And you don't need to now. Dixon's here. You have your life back."

Tuck stared at her in silence.

That was how she saw him? Well, at least he knew the truth. Even after all they'd done together, how hard they'd worked to save clients and accounts, she thought he'd only been biding his time until he could go back to the party circuit.

"I'm free," he agreed between gritted teeth.

"Then, no reason to linger."

He stared hard into her eyes. “No reason at all.”

Unless he counted how he felt about her, how much he wanted to be with her, how hard he wished she’d see something in him besides an irresponsible playboy.

“I’m going to be busy with Dixon,” she said airily. “And with Jade, and with Crystal.”

“I’m going to be busy getting my name back in the tabloids.” As he said it, he willed her to call his bluff.

She didn’t even hesitate. “Good luck with that.”

“Thanks.”

There was nothing left to say. But the last thing he wanted to do was leave.

He wanted to hug her. He wanted to kiss her. At the very least, he wanted to thank her for the help and for the amazing memories.

Instead, he left without a word.

Twelve

Amber missed Tuck, and the hurt was beyond anything she could have imagined. Each day she arrived at the office and promised herself it would be better. She'd think about him less, stop imagining his voice, stop thinking every set of footsteps in the hallway might be his. She was going to get past it.

Jade was home from the hospital and Crystal was adorable. Though the baby wasn't the best sleeper in the world. Amber told herself that living in a state of mild sleep deprivation had to be contributing to her depression. Surely, one man couldn't be the cause of all this.

Dixon had slipped right into the familiarity of his old job. He was definitely in a more upbeat mood, but he was just as efficient as always, no matter what the crisis.

It was coming up on eleven and the phone had been ringing almost constantly. There was a storm in the Atlantic and a major rock slide across one of the main rail lines between Denver and Salt Lake City. Everybody was rerouting and rescheduling.

"The Blue Space file?" Dixon called through the open door of his office.

Amber knew the Blue Space file was in Tuck's office. She'd been avoiding going in there, worried about triggering memories. Not that anything specific had ever happened in his office. They hadn't kissed and they certainly hadn't made love there. Thank goodness, at least, for that.

"I'll get it," she called back.

"They're phoning right after lunch," said Dixon.

"On my way."

She took a bracing breath and stood. She was going to do

this. In fact, she wanted to do this. Maybe it would be a turning point. Maybe she'd built it up to be something it wasn't. She could probably walk in there, get the file, walk back out and realize it was just another room.

She headed down the hall.

Tuck's office door was closed. But she refused to slow down. She reached out, turned the knob, thrust the door open and walked inside.

There, she stopped, gasping a breath, picking up his scent, her brain assailed by memories. Tuck laughing. Tuck scowling. His brows knitted together in concentration.

She could hear his voice, feel his touch and imagine his kiss.

"Amber?" Dixon's voice startled her.

"I'm sure it was on the desk," she said, pushing herself forward.

There was a stack of files on the corner of the desktop and she began looking through them.

"I'm meeting Zachary for lunch," said Dixon.

"Zachary who?" She tried to remember if there was a Zachary connected with Blue Space.

"Zachary Ingles."

She looked up. "Why?"

Dixon moved closer. "I'm trying to get him to come back."

"Why would you do that?"

"Because he's good. And he took a bunch of accounts with him when he left."

"There's nothing good about that."

She'd never liked Zachary. She didn't trust him and she'd been glad to see him leave. The new guy, Samuel Leeds, was much more professional. He was young, but he seemed to be learning fast.

Dixon chuckled. "I know Zachary's not the warmest guy in the world."

Amber continued sorting. It wasn't her place to criticize, and she didn't want to insult Dixon.

"Samuel's a bit too laid-back," said Dixon. "He's inexperienced. A director position isn't the place to learn the ropes."

"He's enthusiastic," said Amber.

"A little too enthusiastic."

Dixon had said the same thing about Gena, the new finance director. He hadn't replaced her yet, but Amber knew he'd been in contact with Harvey.

"Are you going to undo everything Tuck did?" As soon as she asked, Amber immediately regretted the question.

"You mean, am I going to undo the damage?"

She practically had to bite her tongue.

"It must have been bedlam around here." Dixon crossed his arms over his chest.

"Who says that?"

"Harvey, for one."

"Consider the source."

Dixon didn't respond and Amber realized she'd gone too far.

"What did that mean?" asked Dixon, a clear rebuke in his tone.

Amber straightened and squared her shoulders. She was loyal to Tucker Transportation and she'd been appropriately loyal to Dixon. She now found herself feeling some of that loyalty toward Tuck.

"Tuck worked hard," she said.

"I've no doubt that he did."

"He not only worked hard—he succeeded. Yes, Harvey and Zachary bailed. But you should ask yourself what that says about them."

"They couldn't work with Tuck."

"Or they *wouldn't* work with Tuck. Zachary stole your clients. He *stole* them. He was disrespectful to Tuck. He was disloyal to you. He was downright dishonest. And, by the way, he hits on your female employees. Tuck, on the other hand, came in here without the first idea of what to do. He could have bailed. He could have turned and run the other way. But he didn't. He dug in. Even knowing what your father thought of him, and how he'd been treated in the past, and how overwhelming the learning curve turned out to be, he stuck it out. Did you thank him? Did your dad thank him? Did anyone thank him?"

"We paid him."

"He didn't do it for the money. And he didn't do it to save the company. He has pride, Dixon. He had purpose. We won back half the clients and we signed up some more. He worked eighteen-hour days, threw his heart and soul into making sure the company didn't fail while you were off sailing. He hunted far and wide to get Gena and Samuel. Yes, they're both young. But they're well educated. They have some experience. And they're bringing new energy to the company. And that's thanks to Tuck, who was thrown in here without a lifeline."

Amber stopped talking. As she did, the magnitude of her outburst hit her.

"Amber?" Dixon began, clearly baffled by her behavior.

She was instantly overcome with regret. She knew she was about to get fired by the third Tucker Transportation owner. It was going to be a clean sweep.

"Yes," she said in a small voice.

"Did something happen between you and Tuck?"

She ignored the personal implication of the question. "I got to know him." It was an honest answer.

"You got to know him well?" Dixon was watching her carefully.

"Better than before. When he first showed up, I thought the same thing you obviously do—that he was a lazy playboy who was going to fall flat on his face and wouldn't even know it when he did. I wouldn't even help him. I mean, I helped him, of course. But I wasn't going the extra mile like I might have been. But then I saw how hard he worked. He truly was dedicated. And I started to understand that he hadn't chosen to stay away—your father had barred him entry."

"He has an office," said Dixon.

"That's what I said. And he does. But nobody wants him. He understands that full well."

"Amber?"

"What?"

Her fear was gone. Whatever was going to happen was going to happen. But she wasn't about to turn her back on Tuck. He'd worked hard and she wouldn't pretend that he hadn't, even to please Dixon.

"That wasn't my question."

She hesitated. "I know."

"What happened between the two of you?"

"Nothing."

Dixon waited, looking unconvinced.

"Okay, something," she said. "But it's over and done."

Silence settled thick in the air, but she refused to break it. She'd already said too much.

Dixon went first. "Are you in love with Tuck?"

She felt the world shift beneath her feet. "No."

She couldn't be. She wouldn't be. She'd made mistakes with Tuck, but she wouldn't make that one.

"I'm sorry," said Dixon.

"For what?" Was she about to be fired after all?

"That Tuck hurt you."

"He didn't hurt me."

And if he had, she'd get over it. She'd seen what falling for the wrong man could do, *would* do. She wasn't going to do that to herself.

Dixon gave a considered nod. "Okay. Tell me what else you know about Samuel."

"Why?"

"Because you just made an impassioned plea on his behalf. Do you want to drop the ball now?"

She didn't. "He works well with Hope. And I respect Hope. She has her finger on the pulse of social media."

"You think we need social media?"

"That's like asking if you need telephones or computers.

Yes, you need social media. Your father might not have seen it, but you need to think about the next twenty years, not the past twenty years."

"I'll give it some thought," he said.

She couldn't quite let it go. "*It* meaning social media, or keeping Samuel?"

Dixon coughed out a chuckle. "You know, Tuck went to great lengths to impress upon me how loyal you were to me. But what I'm seeing right now is how loyal you are to him."

"I'm not loyal to Tuck."

"Okay."

"I'm only being fair to him."

"Then, I'll be fair to you."

She swallowed. "You won't fire me?"

Dixon looked puzzled. "Fire you for what?"

"Insubordination."

"Is that a euphemism for offering your opinion?"

"In this case, it means offering my opinion forcefully and without provocation."

"That's not what I meant, but you're not fired, Amber. I'd hire fifty of you if I could."

She handed him the Blue Space file. "That was a nice thing to say."

"I'm hoping to win back your loyalty."

"You never lost it."

He glanced around the office. "Then, I can't help but wonder what exactly it was that Tuck gained."

She was about to say *nothing*, but Dixon turned and left her alone.

She stood for a moment, holding the atmosphere, remembering every little thing about Tuck until her heart throbbed and her chest ached, and she felt silent and alone and empty.

Tuck stared at his silent cell phone for a full minute before he slid it back inside his pocket. He was dressed to the nines, had a reservation at the Seaside, followed by tickets to a popular live comedy show, and he planned to end the evening at the Hollingsworth Lounge.

MaryAnn was a great date—bright, bubbly, lots of fun. But Tuck simply didn't have it in him right now. He didn't want to romance MaryAnn or anyone else. He didn't want to dine with them, dance with them or even sleep with them.

He was on the rebound from Amber. He got that, even though they'd barely dated. But the rebound had never hit him like this before.

The front door of the mansion opened and Dixon entered the foyer, doing a double take at the sight of Tuck.

"Hot date?" Dixon asked.

"Just got canceled."

"She get a better offer?"

"Something like that." Tuck wasn't about to tell Dixon that he was the one who'd canceled the date. He'd used a lame excuse of having a headache. As if a normal guy would give up a night with MaryAnn over a headache.

Trouble was, most normal guys hadn't fallen for Amber.

"Are you staying in?" asked Dixon.

"Might as well." Tuck loosened his tie.

"Drink?"

"Sure." Tuck followed his brother into the library.

He purposely sat down across from the chair where Amber had sat in her bare feet and sparkling dress. Then he smiled wistfully at the memory. She was so incredibly sexy with those luscious lips, simmering eyes, smooth shoulders and toned legs. He shifted in his chair.

Dixon handed him a crystal glass with two ice cubes and a shot of single malt. "What?"

"Nothing," said Tuck.

"You're smiling."

"I'm not sorry about the date." Tuck took a drink.

"That's an odd reaction." Dixon sat down.

Tuck gave a noncommittal shrug.

"I was talking to Zachary today," said Dixon.

"Why would you do that?" Tuck wouldn't have given the man the time of day.

"He's interested in coming back."

Tuck didn't bother responding. Dixon knew how he felt about Zachary.

Dixon seemed to give him a moment. "You got any thoughts on that?"

In response, Tuck scoffed. "You don't want to hear my thoughts on that."

"You don't think we should take him back?"

"I think we should drop him off the Michigan Avenue Bridge."

Dixon cracked a smile. "Let's call that plan B."

"Let's." Tuck drank again, pulling for plan B.

"Amber doesn't like him," said Dixon.

"Amber's not stupid."

"No, she's not."

Her image appeared once more in the chair across from Tuck.

"You're smiling again," said Dixon.

"Did she tell you her sister had a baby?"

"When did that happen?"

"Two weeks ago. Just before you got back."

"Is her sister in Chicago?"

Tuck nodded. "She is now." He found himself glancing around the library. "You ever give much thought to the way we grew up?"

"You mean with a controlling father and a distant mother?"

"I mean with gold-plated bathroom faucets."

"The faucets aren't gold-plated," said Dixon. "Though I'm honestly not sure about the dining room chandelier."

"We never worried about having enough to eat. Heck, we never worried about running low on gourmet ice cream."

"Rich people still have problems."

"I know that," said Tuck. "They never would buy me a pony."

He knew Amber's childhood challenges had been on a whole other level. Whenever he thought about that, it left him feeling petty.

"How about the fact that your father thought you were illegitimate?"

Tuck had given that revelation a lot of thought these past few days. It didn't change anything, but it did boost his confidence. He hadn't earned his father's disdain. It had been there all along.

"You said I knew," he said to Dixon. "Why did you think I knew?"

"Because of that night when we overheard."

"What night?"

"In the sitting room, listening at the air vent."

"We did that all the time."

Many nights, after their nanny had put them to bed, they'd sneak out of their room and listen to conversations going on downstairs. Usually they'd do it during parties, but they'd listened in on plenty of their parents' conversations, as well.

"They had a huge shouting match," said Dixon. "Dad accused her of fooling around. She denied it at first, but then admitted it. He said you had someone named Robert's hair and eyes."

Tuck sifted through his brain, but that particular fight didn't stand out. "I don't remember."

"You don't remember learning you might have a different father?"

"I must not have understood. How old was I?"

"Young," Dixon answered thoughtfully. "I said 'wow,' and you said 'wow' back. And I thought you got the meaning."

"I can only guess it went right over my head."

"Wow," said Dixon.

"I'm not going back to the way things were," said Tuck.

For some reason, the path forward crystalized inside his mind.

"Our father can like it or not," he continued. "But it's my company, too. I'm every bit as much his son as you are. I'm not going to be some token partner afraid of voicing my opinion. I'm going to fight you. I'm going to fight hard for what I know is right. Zachary is gone. He stays gone. Harvey, too. Amber..." He hadn't thought his way through what to do about Amber.

"Amber's great," said Dixon.

Tuck looked up sharply. He didn't like the tone of his brother's voice, and he didn't like the expression on Dixon's face. "You stay away from Amber."

"I will not. She's my assistant."

"And that's *all* she is."

"That's far from all she is."

Tuck found himself coming to his feet. "You better explain that statement."

"Explain it how?"

Tuck's voice rose. "What else is she? What is Amber to you? She won't date her boss. She can't date her boss. She would be supremely stupid to date her boss."

"Why?"

"Because it'll end badly for her. That sort of thing always does."

"So you didn't date her?"

"*No*, I didn't date her." Tuck would have dated her. But she'd said no. And she was right to say no.

"And you didn't sleep with her."

"What?" Tuck glared at his brother.

"You're acting pretty jealous for a guy who never dated her."

"I care about her, okay? Sure, I care about her. She's a nice woman. She's a fantastic woman. She's been through a lot, and now she's taking care of her sister. She does that. She takes care of people. She didn't like me, but she helped me anyway. And the whole time you were gone, she had *nothing* but your best interests at heart."

"She's loyal," said Dixon. "You've said that before."

"She is, to her detriment at times."

"Well, for a woman who's supposedly incredibly loyal to me, she sure talks a lot about you."

The statement took Tuck aback. "She does?"

"Almost as much as you talk about her."

"I don't—"

"Give it up, Tuck. You're obsessed with her."

"I like her. What's not to like?"

"You think she's pretty?"

Tuck could barely believe the stupidity of the question. "That's obvious to anybody with a set of eyes."

"You think she's hot?"

"Have you seen her shoes?"

"What shoes?"

"The… You know." Tuck pointed to his feet. "The straps and the heels and the rhinestones and things."

"Never noticed."

"There's something wrong with you, man."

"Why didn't you date her?" Dixon asked.

"Because I was her boss."

"Afterward—now—why don't you ask her out?"

Tuck sat back down and reached for the bottle on the table between them. He took off the cap and poured himself another drink.

"I did," he admitted. "She said no."

Dixon cocked his head. "Did she understand the question?"

"Yes, she understood the question."

"Did she give you a reason?"

"She doesn't trust me. She's got it in her head that I'm still an irresponsible playboy. She doesn't think she can count on me."

Tuck knew why she would feel that way. He also knew she deserved to feel that way. But she was wrong. If she'd give him half a chance, she'd find out she could count on him.

"So that's it? You're not going to fight?"

"How do I fight something like that?"

"How do you fight Dad? How do you fight his perception of you?"

"By standing up for myself. By taking my rightful place in this family."

Dixon cracked a smile. "And?" It was obvious he thought he had Tuck cornered.

"It's not the same thing. I have no rights to Amber at all."

"You do if she's in love with you."

"She's not—" Tuck froze. He gaped at his brother. "What makes you say that?"

"I asked her."

Tuck moved his jaw, struggling to voice the question, terrified to voice the question. "Did she say yes?"

"She said no."

Everything inside Tuck went flat. In that second, he realized he'd held out hope. He'd known it was impossible, but he couldn't seem to stop himself from dreaming.

"But she was lying," said Dixon.

Tuck blinked in bafflement.

"She's in love with you, bro."

"That can't be." Tuck didn't dare hope.

"I'm not saying she's smart or right. I'm just saying she is."

A million thoughts exploded inside Tuck's head. Was it possible? Should he give it another shot? Should he not take her refusal at face value?

"You need to fight," said Dixon. "You're tough, and you're smart and you know what you deserve. Fight Dad, fight Amber if she's being stubborn. Hell, fight me if you think I'm wrong."

Tuck tried but failed to temper his hope. "You are wrong. You're wrong about a lot of things."

"Then, fight me."

"But I hope you're right about this."

"You love her?"

"Yes," said Tuck, knowing it was completely and irrevocably true. He was in love with Amber and he was going to fight for her with everything he had.

Amber rocked Crystal in her arms while Jade worked on an English essay on her laptop. She told herself they were a family now. She had her job back, and the future was bright. Little Crystal was perfect, and she was going to grow up safe and happy, knowing she had a devoted mom and aunt to care for her.

Her gaze strayed to a glossy magazine on the coffee table. *Chicago About Town*. Jade had brought it home with the groceries. There was an inset photo on the bottom left, Tuck with a beautiful blonde woman. She didn't know who it was and it was impossible to know when the photo was taken. But Amber was jealous.

Tuck was back to his old life, while Dixon's words kept echoing inside her head. *Are you in love with Tuck?*

How could she have fallen in love with Tuck? How could she have been so foolish? She had so much going for her right now. Jade was working hard. She was going to pass her equivalency test. She was going to be a great mom.

Amber kissed the soft top of Crystal's head. The future was blindingly optimistic. All she had to do was get Tuck out of her head.

Her chest tightened and her throat seemed to clog.

"Amber?" Jade asked softly.

Amber swallowed. "Yes?"

"What's wrong?"

"Nothing."

Jade rose from her chair. "Is it too much?"

It was. It was far too much. Amber didn't know if she'd be able to get over him. She didn't want to keep fighting her feelings.

"Me and Crystal?" Jade continued. "Are we too much work?"

"What? No. No, honey. It's not you."

"You look so sad."

"I'm just tired."

"No, you're sad."

"I miss him," Amber admitted.

"Tuck?"

"How can I miss him? I know who he is. I know where it was going. But I couldn't seem to talk myself out of it."

Jade moved toward her, sympathy in her expression. "I know how you feel."

"Does it go away?"

A knock sounded on the door.

"Eventually, your head will overtake your heart," said Jade. "Though it can take a while."

Amber didn't like the sound of that. Her head was stronger than her heart, always. It was what had kept her safe and sane all these years. How could it be failing her now?

The knock sounded again and Jade brushed Amber's shoulder on the way to answer it.

Amber hugged her niece tight.

"I'm looking for Amber." Tuck's voice made Amber sit up straight. "Is she home?"

A buzzing started in the center of her brain, radiating to her chest then along her limbs. What was he doing here?

"What do you want?" asked Jade.

"To talk to her."

"Is it about work?"

"Yes."

Amber came slowly to her feet, careful not to disturb Crystal.

"It's okay," she said to Jade.

Jade sighed and opened the door wider.

Amber came forward. "Tuck?"

Jade gathered Crystal from her arms while Tuck smiled at the baby.

"She's beautiful," he said.

"What do you want?" Amber asked.

Tuck met her gaze. “I’m coming to work on Monday.”

The words surprised her.

“Dixon’s contemplating bringing Zachary back,” said Tuck.

“He told me that, too,” said Amber.

“It’s a bad idea.”

“I agree.”

Tuck glanced behind her. “You mind if I come in?”

She hesitated, but she didn’t want to be rude. “Okay.”

“Did you tell him that’s what you thought?” Tuck asked as she shut the door behind them.

“I did. Then I was afraid he might fire me.”

“Dixon’s not going to fire you.”

“He didn’t.” But she’d made a mental note to keep her opinions to herself. She had grown used to being frank with Tuck, but her relationship with Dixon had always been more formal. She had to respect that.

Cooing to Crystal, Jade made her way down the hall, obviously deciding to give them some privacy.

“Are you planning to stop him?” Amber asked. “From rehiring Zachary.”

“I’m going to try,” said Tuck, moving to the middle of the room. “I’m going back, and I’m going to fight for what I want.”

She was puzzled. “Why?”

“Because it’s my company, too.”

“It’s a lot of work.”

Right now, as he had in the past, Tuck had the best of all possible worlds.

“It is,” he agreed.

“You don’t need to do it.”

“I disagree with that. Tucker Transportation can’t run itself.”

“But Dixon—”

“Dixon doesn’t know everything.”

“He knows a lot.”

Tuck frowned. “What do you think of my brother?”

The question struck her as odd. “You know what I think of your brother. We spent weeks discussing what I thought of your brother.”

“We spent weeks trying to keep our hands off each other.”

Amber couldn’t believe she’d heard right.

“Let me put that another way,” he said.

“Good idea.”

“What do you think of me?”

“Right this moment?”

“Right this moment.”

Amber reached down and lifted the magazine, putting the cover in front of his face, reminding herself of exactly who he was.

“What?” He squinted.

“I think you’re exactly what you seem.”

“That’s Kaitlyn.”

“Nice that you remember her name.”

“That’s from last year. At the charity thing. The one for the animals. Pets, not the zoo.”

“The humane society?”

“Yes.”

“Did you have a nice time?”

“Why are you asking? What difference does that make now?”

“Because it’s on the cover of a magazine.”

He stared at her for a long moment. “I’m not dating anyone, Amber.”

“I don’t care.”

But she was lying. She did care. She couldn’t stand the thought of him with another woman. She wanted him for herself and she didn’t know how to stop wanting that.

“You should care,” he said. “You better care.”

“I don’t—”

“I asked you what you thought of me.”

“And I told you.”

He snapped the magazine from her hands and tossed it on the table. "Use words."

Her brain stumbled around. With him standing so close, she found she couldn't lie. "You're not good for me."

"Why not?"

"Don't do this, Tuck."

"Why not?"

"You know I'm attracted to you. You know we have chemistry. But we can't go there again."

"Why not?"

"Why *not*?" she all but shouted.

Why was he determined to make her say it?

"That's what I asked," he said.

"Because it's not enough."

"What would be enough?"

"Stop. Just stop." She wanted him to go away. Her heart was already shredded and he was making it worse.

"Me loving you?" he asked. "Would that be enough?"

His words penetrated and her brain screeched to a halt.

"Would it, Amber?" he asked. "Because I do. I love you. I'm *in* love with you. I want to work with you. I want to date you. I think I even want to marry you. Scratch that. I *know* I want to marry you. Now I'm asking again. What do you think of me?"

She worked her jaw, but no sound came out. "I…uh…"

He cocked his head. "I'm really not sure how to take that."

"You love me?" She couldn't wrap her head around it.

"I love you." He reached out and took her hands in his. "But I'm going to have to insist you answer the question. I swear, Amber, I don't know whether to kiss you or slink out the door."

"Kiss me," she said, joy blooming in her chest.

Tuck's face broke into a broad smile.

"I love you, Tuck. Kiss me, please."

He didn't wait another second. He kissed her deeply, wrapping his arms around her, drawing her close against his body.

"I'll be there for you," he whispered in her ear. "I promise I'll be there for you and for Crystal and for Jade. I'll protect you and fight for you. You can count on me now and forever."

"This doesn't seem real." She let the warmth of his body flow into hers.

"It's real, sweetheart. And it's definitely forever."

* * * * *

Copper Ridge, Oregon's, favorite bachelor is about to meet his match!

If the devil wore flannel, he'd look like Ace Thompson. He's gruff. Opinionated. Infernally hot. The last person Sierra West wants to ask for a bartending job—not that she has a choice. Ever since discovering that her "perfect" family is built on a lie, Sierra has been determined to make it on her own. Resisting her new boss should be easy when they're always bickering. Until one night, the squabbling stops...and something far more dangerous takes over. Ace has a personal policy against messing around with staff—or with spoiled rich girls. But there's a steel backbone beneath Sierra's silver-spoon upbringing. She's tougher than he thought, and so much more tempting. Enough to make him want to break all his rules, even if it means risking his heart...

Read on for this special extended excerpt from ONE NIGHT CHARMER by USA TODAY *bestselling author Maisey Yates.*

CHAPTER ONE

THERE WERE TWO PEOPLE in Copper Ridge, Oregon, who—between them—knew nearly every secret of every person in town. The first was Pastor John Thompson, who heard confessions of sin and listened to people pour out their hearts when they were going through trials and tribulations.

The second was Ace Thompson, owner of the most popular bar in town, son of the pastor and probably the least likely to attend church on Sunday or any other day.

There was no question that his father knew a lot of secrets, though Ace was pretty certain he himself got the more honest version. His father spent time standing behind the pulpit; Ace stood behind a bar. And there he learned the deepest and darkest situations happening in the lives of other townspeople while never revealing any of his own. He supposed, pastor or bartender, that was kind of the perk.

They poured it all out for you, and you got to keep your secrets bottled up inside.

That was how Ace liked it. Every night of the week, he had the best seat in the house for whatever show Copper Ridge wanted to put on. And he didn't even have to pay for it.

And with his newest acquisition, the show was about to get a whole lot better.

"Really?" Jack Monaghan sat down at the bar, beer in hand, his arm around his new fiancée, Kate Garrett. "A mechanical bull?"

"That's right, Monaghan. This is a classy establishment, after all."

"Seriously," Connor Garrett said, taking the seat next to

Jack, followed by his wife, Liss. "Where did you get that thing?"

"I traded it. Guy down in Tolowa owed me some money and he didn't have it. So he said I could come by and look at his stash of trash. Lo and behold, I discovered Ferdinand over there."

"Congratulations," Kate said. "I didn't think anything could make this place more of a dive. I was wrong."

"You're a peach, Kate," Ace said.

The woman smiled broadly and wrapped her arm around Jack's, leaning in and resting her cheek on his shoulder.

"Can we get a round?" Connor asked.

Ace continued to listen to their conversation as he served up their usual brew, enjoying the happy tenor of the conversation, since the downers would probably be around later to dish out woe while he served up harder liquor. The Garretts were good people, he mused. Always had been. Both before he'd left Copper Ridge, and since he'd come back.

His focus was momentarily pulled away when the pretty blonde who'd been hanging out in the dining room all evening drinking with friends approached the aforementioned Ferdinand.

He hadn't had too many people ride the bull yet, and he had to admit, he was finding it a pretty damn enjoyable novelty.

The woman tossed her head, her tan cowboy hat staying in place while her blond curls went wild around her shoulders. She wrapped her hands around the harness on top of the mechanical creature and hoisted herself up. Her movements were unsteady, and he had a feeling, based on the amount of time the group had been here, and how often the men in the group had come and gone from the bar, that she was more than a little bit tipsy.

Best seat in the house. He always had the best seat in the house.

She glanced up as she situated herself and he got a good look at her face. There was a determined glint in her eyes, her brows locked together, her lips pursed into a tight circle. She wasn't just tipsy, she was pissed. Looking down at the bull like it was her own personal Everest and she was determined to conquer it along with her rage. He wondered what a bedazzled little thing like her had to be angry about. A broken nail, maybe. A pair of shoes that she really wanted that was unavailable in her size.

She nodded once, her expression growing even *more* determined as she signaled the employee Ace had operating the controls tonight.

Ace moved nearer to the bar, planting his hands flat on the surface. "This probably won't end well."

The patrons at the bar turned their heads toward the scene. And he noticed Jack's posture go rigid. "Is that—"

"Yes," Kate said.

The mechanical bull pitched forward and the petite blonde sitting on top of it pitched right along with it. She managed to stay seated, but in Ace's opinion that was a miracle. The bull went back again, and the woman straightened, arching her back and thrusting her breasts forward, her head tilted upward, the overhead lighting bathing her pretty face in a golden glow. And for a moment, just a moment, she looked like a graceful, dirty angel getting into the rhythm of the kind of riding Ace preferred above anything else.

Then the great automated beast pitched forward again and the little lady went over the top, down onto the mats underneath. There were howls from her so-called friends as they enjoyed her deposition just a little too much.

She stood on shaky legs and walked back over to the group, picking up a shot glass and tossing back another, her face twisted into an expression that suggested this was not typical behavior for her.

Kate frowned and got up from her stool, making her way over to the other woman.

Ace had a feeling he should know the woman's name, had a feeling that he probably did somewhere in the back corner of his mind. He knew everyone. Which meant that he knew a lot *about* a lot of people, recognized nearly every face he passed on the street. He could usually place them with their most defining life moments, as those were the things that often spilled out on the bar top after a few shots too many.

But it didn't mean he could put a name to every face. There were simply too many of them.

"Who is that?" he asked.

"Sierra West," Jack said, something strange in his tone.

"Oh, right."

He knew the West family well enough, or rather, he knew of them. Everyone did. Though they were hardly the type to frequent his establishment. Sierra did, which would explain why she was familiar, though they never made much in the way of conversation. She was the type who was always absorbed in her friends or her cell phone when she came to place her order. No deep confessionals from Sierra over drinks.

He'd always found it a little strange she patronized his bar when the rest of the West family didn't.

Dive bars weren't really their thing.

He imagined mechanical bulls probably weren't, either. Judging not just on Sierra's pedigree, but on the poor performance.

"No cotillions going on tonight, I guess," Ace said.

Jack turned his head sharply, his expression dark. "What's that supposed to mean?"

"Nothing."

He didn't know why, but his statement had clearly offended Monaghan. Ace wasn't in the business of voicing his opinion. He was in the business of listening. Listening and serving. No one needed to know his take on a damn thing. They just wanted a sounding board to voice their own opinions and hear them echoed back.

Typically, he had no trouble with that. This had been a little slipup.

"She's not so bad," Jack said.

Sierra was a friend of Jack's fiancée, that much was obvious. Kate was over there talking to her, expression concerned. Sierra still looked mutinous. Ace was starting to wonder if she was mad at the entire world, or if something in particular had set her off.

"I'm sure she isn't." He wasn't sure of any such thing. In fact, if he knew one thing about the world and all the people in it, it was that there was a particular type who used their every advantage in life to take whatever they wanted, whenever they wanted it, regardless of promises made. Whether they were words whispered in the dark or vows spoken in front of whole crowds of loved ones.

He was a betting man. And he would lay odds that Sierra West was one of those people. She was the type. Rich, a big fish in the small pond of the community and beautiful. That combination pretty much guaranteed her whatever she wanted. And when the option for *whatever you wanted* was available, very few people resisted it.

Hell, why would you? There were a host of things he would change if he had infinite money and power.

But just because he figured he'd be in the same boat if he were rich and almighty didn't mean he had to like it on others.

HE LOOKED BACK over at Kate, who patted her friend on the shoulder before shaking her head and walking back toward the group. "She didn't want to come sit with us or anything," Kate said, looking frustrated.

The Garrett-Monaghan crew lingered at the bar for another couple of hours before they were replaced by another set of customers. Sierra's group thinned out a little bit, but didn't disperse completely. A couple of the guys were starting to get rowdy, and Ace was starting to think he was going to have to play the part of his own bouncer tonight. It wouldn't be the first time.

Fortunately, the noisier members of the group slowly trickled outside. He watched as Sierra got up and made her way back to the bathroom, leaving a couple of girls—one of whom he assumed was the designated driver—sitting at the table.

The tab was caught up, so he didn't really care how it all went down. He wasn't a babysitter, after all.

He turned, grabbed a rag out of the bucket beneath the counter and started to wipe it down. When he looked up again, the girls who had been sitting at the table were gone, and Sierra West was standing in the center of the room looking around like she was lost.

Then she glanced his way, and her eyes lit up like a sinner looking at salvation.

Wrong guess, honey.

She wandered over to the bar, her feet unsteady. "Did you see where my friends went?"

She had that look about her. Like a lost baby deer. All wide, dewy eyes and unsteady limbs. And damned if she wasn't cute as hell.

"Out the door," he said, almost feeling sorry for her. Almost.

She wasn't the first pretty young drunk to get ditched in his bar by stupid friends. She was also exactly the kind of woman he avoided at all costs, no matter how cute or seemingly vulnerable she was.

"What?" She swayed slightly. "They weren't supposed to leave me."

She sounded mystified. Completely dumbfounded that anyone would ever leave her high and dry.

"I figured," he said. "Here's a tip—get better friends."

She frowned. "They're the best friends I have."

He snorted. "That's a sad story."

She held up her hand, the broad gesture out of place coming from such a refined creature. "Just a second."

"Sure."

She turned away, heading toward the door and out to the parking lot.

He swore. He didn't know if she had a car out there, but she was way too skunked to drive.

"Watch the place, Jenna," he said to one of the waitresses, who nodded and assumed a rather important-looking position with her hands flat on the bar and a rag in her hand, as though she were ready to wipe crumbs away with serious authority.

He rounded the counter and followed the same path Sierra had just taken out into the parking lot. He looked around for a moment and didn't see her. Then he looked down and there she was, sitting on the edge of the curb. "Everything okay?"

That was a stupid question; he already knew the answer.

She looked up. "No."

He let out a long-drawn-out sigh. The problem was, he'd followed her out here. If he had just let her walk out the door, then nothing but the pine trees and the seagulls would have been responsible for her. But no, he'd had to follow. He'd been concerned about her driving. And now he would have to follow through on that concern.

"You don't have a ride?"

She shook her head, looking miserable. "Everyone left me. Because they aren't nice. You're right. I do need better friends."

"Yes," he said, "you do. And let me go ahead and tell you right now, I won't be one of them. But as long as you don't live somewhere ridiculous like Portland, I can give you a ride home."

And this, right here, was the curse of owning a bar. Whether he should or not, he felt responsible in these situations. She was compromised, it was late, and she was alone. He could not let her meander her way back home. Not when he could easily see that she got there safely.

"A ride?" She frowned, her delicate features lit dramatically by the security light hanging on the front of the bar.

"I know your daddy probably told you not to take rides from strangers, but trust me, I'm the safest bet around. Unless you want to call someone." He checked his watch. "It's inching close to last call. I'm betting not very many people are going to come out right now."

She shook her head slowly. "Probably not."

He sighed heavily, reaching into his pocket and wrapping his fingers around his keys. "All right, come on. Get in the truck."

SIERRA LOOKED UP at her unlikely, bearded, plaid-clad savior. She knew who he was, of course. Ace Thompson was the owner of the bar, and she bought beer from him at least twice a month when she came out with her friends. They'd exchanged money and drinks across the counter more times than she could recall, but this was more words than she'd ever exchanged with him in her life.

She was angry at herself. For getting drunk. For going out with the biggest jerks in the local rodeo club. For getting on the back of a mechanical bull and opening herself up to their derision—because honestly, when you put your drunk self up on a fake, bucking animal, you pretty much deserved it. And most of all, for sitting down in the parking lot acting like she was going to cry just because she had been ditched by said jerky friends.

Oh, and being *caught* at what was most definitely an epic low made it all even worse. He'd almost certainly seen her inglorious dismount off the mechanical bull, then witnessed everyone leaving without her.

She'd been so sure today couldn't get any worse.

She'd been wrong.

"I'm fine," she said, and she could have bitten off her own tongue, because she wasn't fine. As much as she wanted to pretend she didn't need his help, she kind of did. Granted, she could call Colton or Madison. But if her sister had to drive all the way down to town from the family estate she would probably kill Sierra. And if she called Colton's house his fiancée would probably kill Sierra.

Either way, that made for a dead Sierra.

She wasn't speaking to her father. Which, really, was the root of today's evil.

"Sure you are. *Most* girls who end up sitting on their behinds at 1:00 a.m. in a parking lot are just fine."

She blinked, trying to bring his face into focus. He refused to be anything but a fuzzy blur. "I am."

For some reason, her stubbornness was on full display, and most definitely outweighed her common sense. That was probably related to the alcohol. And to the fact that all of her restraint had been torn down hours ago. Sometime early this morning when she had screamed at her father and told him she never wanted to see him again, because she'd found out he was a liar. A cheater.

Right, so that was probably why she was feeling rebellious. Angry in general. But she probably shouldn't direct it at the person who was offering a helping hand.

"Don't make me ask you twice, Sierra. It's going to make me get real grumpy, and I don't think you'll like that." Ace shifted his stance, crossing his arms over his broad chest—she was pretty sure it was broad, either that or she was seeing double—and looked down at her.

She got to her wobbly feet, pitching slightly to the side before steadying herself. Her head was spinning, her stomach churning, and she was just mad. Because she felt like crap. Because she knew better than to drink like this, at least when she wasn't in the privacy of her own home.

"Which truck?" she asked, rubbing her forehead.

He turned, not waiting for her, and began to walk across the parking lot. She followed as quickly as she could. Fortunately, the lot was mostly empty, so she didn't have to watch much but the back of Ace as they made their way to the vehicle. It wasn't a new, flashy truck. It was old, but it was in good condition. Better than most she'd seen at such an advanced age. But then, Ace wasn't a rancher. He owned a bar, so it wasn't like his truck saw all that much action.

She stood in front of the passenger-side door for a long moment before realizing he was not coming around to open it for her. Her face heated as she jerked open the door for herself and climbed up inside.

It had a bench seat. And she found herself clinging to the door, doing her best to keep the expansive seat between them as wide as possible. She was suddenly conscious of the fact that he was a very large man. Tall, broad, muscular. She'd known that, somewhere in the back of her mind. But the way he filled up the cab of a truck containing just the two of them was much more significant than the way he filled the space in a vast and crowded bar.

He started the engine, saying nothing as he put the truck in Reverse and began to pull out of the lot. She looked straight ahead, desperate to find something to say. The silence was oppressive, heavy around them. It made her feel twitchy, nervous. She always knew what to say. She was in command of every social situation she stepped into. People found her charming, and if they didn't, they never said otherwise. Because she was Sierra West, and her family name carried with it the burden of mandatory respect from the people of Copper Ridge.

She took a deep breath, trying to ease the pressure in her chest, trying to remove the weight that was sitting there.

"What's your sign?" Somehow, her fuzzy brain had retrieved that as a conversation starter. The moment the words left her mouth she wanted to stuff them back in and swallow them.

To her surprise, he laughed. "Caution."

"What?"

"I'm a caution sign, baby. And it would be in your best interest to obey the warning..."

Don't miss what happens when Sierra doesn't heed his advice in
ONE NIGHT CHARMER
by USA TODAY *bestselling author Maisey Yates!*

COMING NEXT MONTH FROM

Available May 10, 2016

#2443 TWINS FOR THE TEXAN

Billionaires and Babies • by Charlene Sands

When Brooke McKay becomes pregnant after a one-night stand with a sexy rancher, she tracks him down to discover he's a widower struggling with toddler twins! Can she help as his nanny before falling in love—and delivering her baby bombshell?

#2444 IN PURSUIT OF HIS WIFE

Texas Cattleman's Club: Lies and Lullabies

by Kristi Gold

A British billionaire and his convenient wife wed for all the wrong reasons...and she can't stay when he won't open his heart, even though their desire is undeniable. But now that she's pregnant, the stakes for their reunion are even higher...

#2445 SECRET BABY SCANDAL

Bayou Billionaires • by Joanne Rock

Wealthy football star Jean-Pierre despises the media. When rumors fly, he knows who to blame—the woman who's avoided him since their red-hot night together. His proposition: pretend they're a couple to end the scandal. But Tatiana has secrets of her own...

#2446 THE CEO'S LITTLE SURPRISE

Love and Lipstick • by Kat Cantrell

CEO Gage Branson isn't above seducing his ex, rival CEO Cassandra Clare, for business, but when he's accused of the corporate espionage threatening Cassie's company, it gets personal fast. And then he finds out someone's been hiding a little secret...

#2447 FROM FRIEND TO FAKE FIANCÉ

Mafia Moguls • by Jules Bennett

Mobster Mac O'Shea is more than willing to play fiancé with his sexy best friend at a family wedding. But it doesn't take long for Mac to realize the heat between them is all too real...

#2448 HIS SEDUCTION GAME PLAN

Sons of Privilege • by Katherine Garbera

Ferrin is the only one who can clear Hunter's name, and Hunter isn't above using charm to persuade her. He says he's only interested in the secrets she protects—so why can't he get his enemy's daughter out of his mind?